About a Boy, Stories

Benjamin Anderson

About a Boy, Stories
First Edition

Published by:
Biographical Publishing Company
95 Sycamore Drive
Prospect, CT 06712-1493
Phone: 203-758-3661
Fax: 253-793-2618
e-mail: biopub@aol.com

Publisher's Cataloging-in-Publication Data

Anderson, Benjamin
About a Boy, Stories / by Benjamin Anderson.
1st ed. POD-I
p. cm.
1. Title. 2. Short stories. 3. Fiction. 4. Humor.
Dewey Decimal Classification: 808.831 Short Stories
BISAC Subjects:
   FIC029000 FICTION / Short Stories
   FIC016000 FICTION / Humorous / General

To Kris

Also by Benjamin Anderson

Fiction

Sirens of Morning Light
Middle of the Road
Belonging

Non-fiction

Eighteen In Cross-country Odyssey
Quick Quirks, A Quick Book
On a Fallen Wave
Below the Fold

Contents

The Pineapple

She stood at the end of the hallway—is it that simple? So what if that's not enough? So what if love and birth keeps us inert and spinning in space? Can't there be something more that keeps us all going? I ask because somewhere between trash can music and—have you seen those unmistakable (in being) but mistakenly given smiles received to the person standing in some assumed to be emptied spot yet occupied by a fella, a brotha sista sorta, the kind of teenage giving knowing, damn (could I?) if I call it a flower. Yes, an American must not just wake but breathe those fragrances on a Monday morning. Grab that hair gel.

Fumes of a trail-bound life swirled somewhere between buildings and the receding glaciers of the mind. Then the trees shot up. Suburbia was man's moderation between ferocious nature and ferocious humanity. Tornadoes need not billow like mother birds need not kill their infected young. Crooks need not fire guns like women need not scream to constrain their young in Suburbia. Suburbia, the greatest park on planet Earth.

The Pineapple sighed by the bathroom mirror, let that fume rise as he stroked the piles up, then as a great partition let two curves fall upon respective ears. Extreme as highest, the hair provided the only safeguard to hardest, practiced eyes in the mirror that eventually ebbed into cushy cowardice or weariness if possible on any days that include a Monday.

"Have a good day," Pineapple. His mother instructed.

Ye-haw, and the mother becomes a sociology branch of family separate from the cultural Pineapple. But the sighs of law remain final so that those groaning gears of a bus, adorning stop sign, hint him that order and government yet textbooks and various godlike authorities remain important, oh yes they do.

Sit down, shut up, and get quiet.

Or stand up, applaud, and swing your shoes in the air! Clap those ped pacers over brethren's hair and rejoice teenage spirit with shared practicality.

The officials are closed for business. Open seat, third on the right.

"Hey, Pineapple."

And he knew to sit instead by him, given THE name.

Backpack over shoulder. Is it one strap, two strap? Bow head, raise head? Pineapple searched the truth between Dr. Seuss and Creed ("Faceless Man":

Because I stand Lord I stand against the faceless man something something something something something something again I stand something something something something)—

"Don't offend me with that one. C'mon, man."

Pineapple put his headphones down.

"There's a difference between artists and composers. Who do these 'artists' think they are anyhow? Why must they paint with one constricted language when music should be universal?"

He blinked to his friend's saddened face. "Shoehorn."

Reacting to the name: "WHY THE" (something else something something something something)

His name was The Shoehorn, and long has neighbor friend inquired the other end, requiring that name. Hard-worked, patient application, and his request demanded that his Mohawk become ferocity, the prickly feathered wing thrust into the air. But a spectacle of the hallway one day and with three bystanders sneaking looks, Pineapple (with one more, hearto hereto) bid him turn head from swinging profile to front, and the triangular spade, running broad shovel at temples to the tippy top, demanded him be appropriated as The Shoehorn.

"The name doesn't speak anything but true like you do, Shoehorn."

But The Pineapple himself was one more, an all-American for every American. Adaptable. In tuxedo and tie he made the business look good as hair tipped down to the honest eyes. In jeans and tie-dye he will fake those thick glasses and slip into a family reunion picture of the 60's, bordering conservative 50's, hinting the authentic coloring of history that the 70's should begin to know. With slack jeans and slack shirt he will survive the casual stroll through the day, this universal Pineapple.

And one more.

He had a stately girlfriend, faring long hair, longing eyes, but so long be not as so near to Pineapple. She was the most unrealistic business woman with a tongue of a tie and church pants, daddy's hundreds of thousands in her pockets, pearl white smile and hardened crust and tender belly and inquisitive eyes.

Not her.

"How're you doing, Cantaloupe?"

A typical man of the 00's Here's Looking At You Era, a Navy cut cut cut (noun, verb, word to throw you off), defined the earning into the rank of Kernel Cantaloupe. But just The Cantaloupe. Private, after all. Some friendly doctors equated in neighborhood conversation by submitting "Mr. Such and Such says so" rather than "Dr. Sir irrevocably pronounces." Wear that degree! Or: Join our club!

"Well, that one went well," Cantaloupe said.

"Do you mean the day—"

"Or the sameness?" Pineapple inserted to amend Shoehorn.

"The sameness," Cantaloupe clarified.

"Sameness."

"Sameness?"

"Sameness!"

"*Sameness.*"

"Shut up!"

"That's not the same."

"Who're you?"

"Wouldn't you like to know." From the sleek gray of the Cantaloupe and the partition of the Pineapple did they view this speaker. But the high Shoehorn would still prevail. "What are we doing?"

"This one first," said Cantaloupe. "We're going home on these buses, straight to our corridors, then straight to bed."

Shoehorn reflected, "The bed part has always been all right. To child or zesty desiring passion. Damn. Where's a holiday when it isn't Christmas? Do we conform to the nation's holidays or can we make our own?"

"You mean you don't want to ride home on the bus," Pineapple ventured.

"That's right."

"Well, we're gonna swing by... so she can swing by... and pick us up."

And she swung by where they swung by so they might drive into one sunset. Pounding on the power windows, thumping to radio's 104, shaking fro on beats two and four, and "Yeah, yeah!" past the once classroom principalities, all did laud her car to the turn out of school, a path known mostly to lead to the real world.

"Ah." Pineapple improved his nose bridge lifting parallel to the front windshield. His eyes trailed to her. His fingers tickled her shoulder. His mouth tightened. "No tie? Ahh… you look good when you wear one."

"Field hockey is tomorrow."

"Yes."

Back passengers shared a gaze equaled by Cantaloupe's frigid leaning away from the back-comforting seat and Shoehorn's cautious cowering away from the fro-crushing ceiling. "Frock!" Cantaloupe addressed.

"You'll always be a Frock to me," Shoehorn stated.

A glance to the mirror and she flirted, "I wear my frock proudly everyday."

"What?!"

Once ago, trite away, FROCK: a woman's or child's dress. "But wait. Frock could mean a guy's dress too or even a friar's habit," Shoehorn speculated with finger thrust upon dictionary. To comply in the mentioning of it later this historic day, Cantaloupe related, "But there's only one Frock we know." She was a most unrealistic epitome of a woman. So down on Shoehorn knees and Cantaloupe knees and with her embracing smile, Pineapple watched over this life, this Frock in his capable hands.

"Get off the road, dorks. Hey!" A double honk, the horn blared. "A-hah—little runts," the mouth spelled from his sports Sedan. Snickers polluted his back car seat while jokes cracked wide as this anonymous smile. "You gotta admit," Frock, "I'm better than them."

"Big Teeth! Get out of town!" Cantaloupe called.

A hollow gape filled the self-consciousness of flashy whites. The green started him, the engine fired, and a "Ha—ha!" belched from the fumes, but Frock yielded as he cut them off and abandoned them in his wake. With sight comprehensible at 0 mph, past company bit the scorn of sign language, waving them away.

"Hate him. Perish," the grim Cantaloupe sentenced. "Frock," he addressed once more, "let's turn around."

"Are you letting him get to you?" Shoehorn demanded.

No, his gestures sighed. "We're out here. Let's make a purpose to it, because you know after we go home—we must return to school tomorrow."

And they swung by where ninety-nine cents remained a way of life. Shoehorn prescribed, "Mph! Feel the bump in the back of the throat, mph! mph! and make the jump with ninety-nine cents to freedom."

"Don't tell me that at the last minute."

Cantaloupe thumbed the back of his ear lobe, then realized his being watched. "Wha-at?"

"I almost squealed my wheels on that turn!"

"Okay, sorry," he hurried.

Pineapple drew his hand to his mouth and away.

"Ah, but you were close, and we were enjoying it."

Down Frock turned the volume and off.

"Don't get me wrong. I appreciate the quiet."

In the moment Frock conceded.

"What would you like today?"

Make it a Mac, Jack, with plenty of lead, gutted to store pickle relish for your needy banger wanger thanger. Off the furthest parking lot space, allow one car door for each person to open or lean on and two hoods for joiners.

"Ah-ah-h. Ah ah." With back and back foot against car door, Cantaloupe raised the burger empirically. "What you doing? The other car door away from your seat?"

"C'mon. Cantaloupe, you know the words." He lifted his finger pads to her shirt cuffs, crossing his Pineapple with her Frock.

Cantaloupe with words molded down, "Hold the cheese and bologna. Starved elopement." Assigning conviction in eviction for the cause, gravity mounting on the other side three to one, he threw the ratio overboard into a non-existent right side of the car where 0/4 was a mathematical theorist's questioning of the right side's existence. By Shoehorn he parked his back on the car door.

Pineapple evaded his friend's gaze but met halfway in words, "And isn't it strange? Cantaloupe saying elopement. Yours would be a Cantaloupement."

"The Cantalouping," Shoehorn envisioned.

"That's right, the Cantalouping." Cantaloupe

spelled, "For those who touch these knuckles, the kiss goodbye."

"Easy."

"I've got a temper. You can kiss them, or they will kiss you."

"What about that shared practicality of teenage benevolence?"

The heads of Pineapple and Frock swiveled on the base of their jointed circle of arms. As one faucet of teenage circumvention from the real, they with eyes implored what institutes would back them if cultures will bear rules like civilizations.

"Speaking of 'ences,' we've got a lot—violence, ambivalence, to take it several ways," Cantaloupe clarified. "Depends which tense you're living in."

Shoehorn resumed in pronouncing, "We have the opportunity to do something outrageously weird, not to fear rules but break them in an ostentatious way."

"Work those words. Say 'parameters' or we'll think Ten Commandments breaking."

"When you see a student in a rabbit costume biking down the school hallway, you'll know we've all been saved."

"And 'I don't know,' and 'what the heck!' if it's you saying it, but I like what you're saying," Cantaloupe defined and in continuation demanded down the culture stream of a body party, "are you children all right?"

"You're both English majors," bestowed Pineapple.

"I declare you both sucklings. Sucking on the greens that, like them, you might age bearably."

"You two break fears, not rules. I don't envy what you are," Shoehorn hurried to help them.

Infatuated mists missed the rule breaking and swirled around them, love breaking free.

"They're most benevolent beings," Cantaloupe allotted in pity for them.

The fumes of chicken nuggets aroused them, and, stink their breath, the salty, greasy, clashing French Fries swirled and caught her throat with her hips, causing him to graze her lips and chomp trenchantly through his tongue.

"Ah! Ooo!"

"Most pitiful," Cantaloupe said, then averting to the aversion. "Big Teeth?"

"Naw," Shoehorn related. "A school group."

In store away coupled teens with electronics removed, two more teased a sign treason to invention like their reactive high-pitched laughter, and behind the car windshield an eyeball pervaded the empty road.

"No left turn," Cantaloupe defended.

With car humming up to the stop, the driver scoffed one sign and then the other. Grinding the gears leftward, he skidded into oncoming traffic until he cleared the interfering jeep, then sped up.

"He's a criminal, not a disobedient servant," Shoehorn related.

Shared hands twined Frock's car key around its

chain free hanging.

But Pineapple could release grasp of her, and when he did, find another day. Venting gasps heralded the rumble over roads, a locomotive of commotion, so violent that when he toppled into the entrance, the wheels kept rounding. Chums hold the door, "Thank you," hold the door, hold the door, "thank you," hold the door—"hey, hold the doooooooooor!" Between crushing shoulders the resilient Pineapple bobbed past the rush with a, "Where did Shoehorn go?" and started banging down the hallway. "Hey."

"Hey," awareness spoke from that boy crouching against the lockers.

Down another passage and up the inside picture locker wall, Pineapple separated the girls to pinpoint, "There's the Byzantine Empire."

"Where?"

"Right below your picture of the opening flower," Pineapple hinted, then gathered to another immediately, "Look at this person! The fro, the glasses. Awesome, man, awesome."

Enlightened counter parties sponged his hair biscuits while lighted glass shielded his eyes as Pineapple danced past the barrier walks of every cultural storm. "Hi, hello," Pineapple acknowledged to the decorated suburbanites and marvel of the most diverse group.

Before him trotting, a guy clopped his hands, and beside, a girl averted her eyes. Clinging his arms, one to each individual, and hugging them together, Pineapple related, "You know, life is love."

"Creep," she vented.

"Don't creep but hurry to confess it. Count each person as a whole individual, not a division of a mind. She has your time. He has your time. Let's make use of the day."

Pineapple put her shirt tag down and, patting the spikes of the guy's hair, shuffled past.

"Good day." Pineapple bowed to the Indian tribe, cross-legged by the lockers. "Hey, get me one of those," Pineapple commanded while passing Hackey Sack 101.

Gracing the social stratosphere, Pineapple floundered down the arteries of the school to discover where students dogged out by locked doors wait. Dan and Danielle must meet here outside homeroom every day, coincidental of course until Vince has something to tell Danielle. Where a student asided a teacher, Pineapple with shoe tip trekked a turn about the forty-inch circumference of the floor respective to him. "Ah, man."

Retiring from sight-filled soaring, not he but the law persuaded him to empty his words and deposit his rump into homeroom. Against the seat backing, Pineapple hitched his hips in pursuing haphazard daydreams and consented metabolically through his metaphysical self to slip into slapdash lovemaking. Entertaining pleasurable women figures, he molded them like a smoke.

Then after homeroom while clonking down the stairwell, a most mischievous sight when he saw the girl's deep breasts hid behind the sorrow contained on her face. Fastened hopes must gleam on those glittery stars, hanging on heavy eyelashes, toward the many poses couples struck by lockers. Pineapple only prayed aspirations be her own.

Sustenance without the substance of youth he cannot find, exploring the square root only when en route to a block away from home, a diner off the plaza of the grand suburban suite. Sweet nostalgia, though innately passing periods one through four and another into five forward, returned him to forever silent slumber only rebuked to the cause of day in those who nodded similarly, only eventually against those who frayed from the purpose.

"Look at baggy boy here."

In Pineapple's face a thrust finger daunted him an inch from his nose, then wavered across the other crowd in the hallway. Satirically mitigating the familiar teacher's performance, an execution of finger waving this scamp danced in and out of peoples' faces. Pineapple recognized the mock-up, constructed in teenage revelry, and joined the rambunctious laughter rising. Then past retained a memory and departed him from the crowd when he recognized them, the school group from yesterday.

"Hey, get baggy pants boy here."

The jumping finger crossed the eyebrows, but the boy unfamiliar did not like it and pushed him away. Sardonically he darted an insistent finger inward pointing, critical of baggy pants without restitution.

"What's going on here?" Cantaloupe demanded with immediacy.

While the school group castigated the boy, actions multiplied and shot fear and hysterics into the thickening crowd, entrapping him double-layered. The critic crushed opposing baggy pants against the wall, and his group added blow upon blow.

Cantalouping, he elbowed through the crowd and to temper the insurgents administered the kiss of those who cannot elope, backhanding the bodies to sever clenched teeth and fists. Pineapple joined Cantaloupe and thrust baggy pants from the revelers back into the uniform crowd.

"Where'd he go? Wait'll I get my hands on!"

"Calm down."

The antagonist's words sank deeper than his own, and though Cantaloupe considered breaking his enemy's jaw with the words, Cantaloupe drank reason, which was sacrificial inaction, until his words calmed his enemy. With opportunity gone, the rebellious youth vanished before written under constructs of law.

"What?   What's there to see?!" Pineapple demanded.

Through the gaping crowd Pineapple pushed past with Cantaloupe following the way to fifth period class. At the empty space where the Big Bang fired and refused to return, the onlookers shrugged their shoulders but assumed expert status to newcomers who flushed the abandoned area, asking.

"What happened?" Shoehorn asked, stopping them.

"What I wish I didn't see," Pineapple responded.

"Who'd you see?"

"The ones who burned the 'no left.'"

"Oh, the scofflaws!"

"We don't have anything left." Cantaloupe coaxed the knuckles and nubbed their tips with a sore palm. "Oh, that we have to endure them. Fear of them causes adults to fear too much else—us."

Pineapple furnished the hand, masking his clean-shaven chin, and commanded the hinging gesture and said, "Let me tell you everything. About a boy and a dream. Oh, they so cruelly wrought impatience for power. Oh, in the stead of power, instead I would offer my capable hands. But when they hop down the walk, throwing their hands and venting the know-how! oh, how they offer no safe alternative to what they accuse." To clarify his just, separate cause, Pineapple pleaded, "I see fragmentation of law as the means of its study. Purpose of law, to safeguard people? Okay, then law, do not harm me, even if my bedazzlement in this day requests of you a favor. Is it illegal to wrap these hallways in belated birthday paper?"

"Oh, how we'll forget this day," Shoehorn detested.

"But only if we capitalize its defeat of conformists and anarchists as one of the many," Pineapple explained.

"Don't hate," Cantaloupe related.
"Just do the fro! Do the fro, fro, fro—do the fro!"

The Shoehorn

*Feel better.   There, how's that?
Sleep well. Eat your vegetables. But you
obviously prefer not to eat your
vegetables. Look at the news today where
victory accompanies the photo finish. The
line beneath the picture will read the
glory of it all, he didn't eat his vegetables.
For what are you looking, how to solve
life like a distance measurement?   You
think life should be like a picture. It's all
perfect then, you say. But it's too safe for
me. Live on, people, go, pack your bags,
leave them behind, hike the trail, jump
over yonder, burp on high.   I laugh at
picture perfect you with all the raw
motions and emotions that really illustrate
life! No moment is safe from time, but
that doesn't mean one should take its
picture and let it die with a corny smile.
What were you trying to attain to be so
secure? Life should be dynamic. Be glad
for so much. Just don't take that picture.
Bounce all over the stagnant atmosphere.
Make it alive again. Make it happy you.*

Straight edges turned ninety-degree corners to mark the wooden bounds of home. A room, a door, a sink top, and a mirror matched the idol of construction, a hexahedron. Dissimilar objects like foam cups to human eye attained irrational features that blended together abnormally. The cloud of a blanket in morning gained a mischievous face with six teeth, and so did the flowers on a shower curtain merge in mind to become birds or puppets. Imaginary these objects became against the primary example of construct, hexahedrons to the stars. The dull, new daylight shrouded the stars, adding a slow, low tone of blue and gray that penetrated the window squares.

The Shoehorn worked within the constricted limits of the mirror. Judging the distance between the walls, he posed into the mirror a sloppy judo kick for the someday salvation of a princess, a furry rabbit, or a cookie crumb pie, toiling again around the restricted boundaries. The Shoehorn snapped his eyelids like a photo shoot of his melancholy form. A grain of a blade of his chicken wing, thrust into the air, erred most maniacally, a smudge in the mirror that continued over to his shocked eyes and drooping mouth.

Only he could wonder what he tried to obtain with a finished, polished, laminated, and plastered picture. The Shoehorn braided the delinquent blades together and laughed in the face of that mirrored image to forever break its formal pose. Where his left cheek would be to others, Shoehorn saw his right cheek in the mirror, so he abandoned the querulous human perspective that delayed objectivity to the waking of another day and sauntered down the stairs.

He grabbed all the milk and cereals and plopped into his seat. Unclasping the box tops, Shoehorn reviewed the magical cereal quest. "Cheerios" to the cultural "Cheerleaders" of a previous decade. Captain Crunch slayed the Rice Krispies elfs (Snap! Crackle! Pop!) just before the crazy craving for Honeycomb (Me want Honeycomb!) distracted the leprechaun (That's me Lucky Charms!) from taming Tony the Tiger (They're grrrrrreat!) while AlphaBits (Marshmallow bits for you and me!) spelled the terms of truce with Honeynut Cheerios (Part of this complete breakfast). The sugar-topped daily pyramid of cereals toppled over the cereal bowl. The human indulgence could not contain the prescribed amount that businesses with memory techniques reminded their customers to eat in order to sell them. Around the high-walled cereal bowl a moat buoyed Honey Nut Chex until the barred Shredded Wheat retreated to neighboring vicinities.

"Is that your complete breakfast?" his father questioned from the archway into the kitchen.

"Honey Nut Cheerios," Shoehorn mechanically replied.

"I could make you some real food."

"Nah. I'm sold to these cereals." Shoehorn scooped the cereal bits into his mouth. "Yeah, hey, how're you doing, Dad?"

"Good."

"Good, very good, very well, okay. You'll have a good day at work, then?"

"I always try."

Shoehorn prowled around the kitchen, armed with the remnants of his cereal. Into the garbage he dumped the soggy cereal bits, parting the milk and bowl and spoon to refrigerator and countertop and sink respectively. In the living room he hiked his backpack on back.

"You have a good day at school," Shoehorn.

"You too, Dad."

"Stay out of trouble."

"Ahnngh," Shoehorn detested, swiveling on his feet. He fired another grunt, and then he pivoted with a louder whinny until the hinges of the door wailed as he jaunted into the early morning cold. Wondering what yesterday's reasoning accomplished as he toted his bookbag to the stop, Shoehorn baffled at what adults sometimes did to become so old.

Shoehorn's eyes lifted, glancing over a peppy individual, adorned with headphones and wiry eyes, a patron of the stop. "You wear a backpack just like any of us," Shoehorn muttered against this individual's flare for bravado. And truly now he saw the backpacks mounted on all their backs except for one girl who held her books out front. But he passed speculation of his conformity and waited for his chariot to come.

And when it did, a cultural vehicle of yellow armoring, he climbed up, passing about five blasting headphones before reaching his seat and again plopping down.

Out of a haze Shoehorn caught The Pineapple, who waved to him with two fingers off his right backpack strap.

"Blah, blah, blah," Shoehorn relented as Pineapple sat with him. "Blah!... Blah!... Blah blah, blah!" Shoehorn joined the music. "That's all I hear. Hey. Hey!" Shoehorn alerted the person in front of him. "I've heard that melody twenty-four damn times! Turn it off!"

"No!"

"Don't you get it? They're trying to *sell you* that melody."

The boy with the headphones turned to put them back on.

"Wait. I'm trying to level with you here, kid. No one can be that depressed to listen to that kinda cheese."

"Why won't you let me listen to my own damn music?"

"Because I'm worried about you. You see, the music group you're listening to, they're trying to sell you a feeling. Turn off the lyrics. Hear the instruments. Then there's nothing."

"I'll turn it down. Just shut up."

"Thank you."

The crashing four-four time of the music dwindled to a whimper. Shoehorn strained his eyes. The Pineapple socked him hard on the shoulder.

"Hey. I'll get you too."

"You're doing pretty well this morning."

"Yeah. But the next set of headphones I see, I'll shoot."

"Too much noise for ya?"

"Ya—and that's the problem. They call it music. Musicians call themselves artists. But few of these pupils of rock get past the cheese, what I call the pulp of this pop society. Basso ostinato, sure, but it climbs up to the melody and strangles it; then louder, louder!"

"What's this basso ostinato?"

"That's when the bass part continuously plays the same set of a few notes over and over. It holds the melody together usually so instrumentalists know which part of the measure they are on."

"Sorry for interrupting."

"Transcribe all music to one instrument. Play that instrument. Then you'll know which music is real." Shoehorn sighed. He watched the trees whipping past, solitary monuments that marked frugal homes of prosperity. "Human emotions were meant to be complex. Unfortunately, human reason delays that, and kids get caught up in their pride of what they're damning to hell. Music can be complex and wonderful. It should be."

The Pineapple paused a moment to soak it all up. Shoehorn meanwhile receded from gestures or words, and Pineapple worried that Shoehorn, while venting his impassioned words, drained certainty. Premature to idolizing past words, Pineapple resumed the conversation. "I don't often hear you address rock with such a general term. Usually you address individual kinds of modern music like... grunge or something."

"How's that?"

"Well, I guess we've reached pop culture now, right?"

Shoehorn shuddered. "Acid, Grunge, Techno, Fusion—give it something better than Pop. They even try Rap."

Pineapple speculated, "Mash, Grime, Sewage—why don't you add music types like these?"

Shoehorn laughed out loud. "Sewage?!" In hearing himself, he adjusted his volume. "Yeah. That's what we should call everything else. You're right. Well, okay. I think we've given these students of violent music a lesson that'll give them nightmares for days to come. Phrased a different way, my words would make a lot of sense to a lot of different people. I'd have to change what I said each time, slightly. A lot of people really have particular musical tastes."

"You beat me."

"I've said all that can be said."

"Go home."

"Why?"

"Go home. Are you deaf?"

"Naw. I've just been listening to music."

"At least you can still call it that."

"Maybe I shouldn't. Another set of headphones?

He dies!"

"Watch out."

"What are we, the soulless?"

"Just the preoccupied."

"Afraid to be bored or easy-going, perhaps." The Shoehorn groaned. "Say one more word and I'll silence you. I'll give you another lecture."

The Pineapple offered him hopeful eyes but danced them past him and out the window.

Negotiating road space with other drivers, the bus reeled wide turns and then docked by the school sidewalk. The Shoehorn and The Pineapple filed off the bus, captivated by its spongy seats and numerous windows as they did go. They walked sneakily and sideways to the school entrance, exploded through the doors where hall monitors spotted them, and hobnobbed with these hired hands while they all employed the words "model student" as the necessary clincher of every statement. Affirming the omen of their meeting this day, The Pineapple and The Shoehorn dashed beyond the summoning voices into the network of the school.

In a frenzy they swept by the halls perpendicular to the one they travel, and they aimed a unique sound or pose into each one. Shoehorn did the distraught scientist. Pineapple did the pigeon wagon puller.

The force of the motion of the back of a hand on an arm of a person on the case of his target blocked Shoehorn as his other arm's hand's finger's tip pointed at Pineapple, and he addressed, "You've been out of my sight too long. What's going on?"

"Cantaloupe," Pineapple replied, "it's like time travel to know where we've been."

"That much of history elapsed since yesterday?"

"Could we possibly relive the hours?" Shoehorn speculated.

"… Well, you've stumped me," Cantaloupe concluded. "What's that bluish blemish on your shoulder?"

Shoehorn eyed the particle. "It's my pet peeve. 'Hello! I'm a speck of dust!'"

"That kid is pure potential."

"What? He's not going anywhere," Pineapple observed.

"Dare you defy his possibility?"

"He should be kinetic. Come on, Shoehorn. Demonstrate your foghorn to him."

Shoehorn put in, "Weather's terrible!"

"But the occasion is right," Cantaloupe commended.

"Then here we go and why are you here and why is this day and why not?" Pineapple improved upon the confusion, offering them forward movement.

On a trek down the farther hallways, they encountered fewer students, but to the things of trash cans, windows, doorknobs, candy wrappers, and ceiling lights they more attended. These ordinary objects sparked their ornery ambitions. In their youthful pursuit of the tangibles, everything jumped out at them. They responded, attaching to them every intangible fancy in their heads.

Cantaloupe indicated the clock on the wall and leapt at it. For a moment in time, he was time, exerting his arms in the formation of the seven and eight.

Shoehorn chuckled and stated, "Yeah, but apart from that optimistic impression, this is when I get up." Both arms dangled limp and perpendicular to the ground.

"Ah, the waking moment. What these authorities make us do!" Pineapple conjugated. "We should wake at a time more appropriate." Stretching his arms parallel to the horizontal floor, he yawned, and then he explained, "I can't stretch or yawn at 6:30, but given some time to warm up like this, 9:15 would be okay."

"What an explanation," Shoehorn commended. "We must be a shared spirit of teenage wonderment because both me and Cantaloupe, I'm sure, like you, thought the same. Sleep! Is wonderment!"

"In turn I follow your explanation, for otherwise, I would be surprised that Cantaloupe discovered the first mirth."

"Delight?" Cantaloupe inquired. "Then those ceiling lights should be the second mirth. The many!"

"If only the daylight outside could be."

Students, socializing in the halls, reacted instantaneously to the summon to homeroom, and the tone that commanded them was not human, though human institution backed it.

"The bell! We've come such a long way, and now

it's such a long way to return," The Cantaloupe remarked. He saluted them and lobbed himself along the path to homeroom.

Pineapple and Shoehorn moved out of the way as certain others scampered past. The will that heeded the school bell was human, their own. Casually Pineapple and Shoehorn strolled to homeroom, observing both the pupils who moved and rebels who stayed.

"Come on," Pineapple! "Let's go," Shoehorn!

"Chief Suhr, how—"

The principal of a principle notion interrupted, "Don't be late to homeroom."

Shoehorn continued, "Wow! How can you judge us like this? Yeow! Now, remember, you're on our side, right?"

Chief Suhr established one embodiment of power, taking form in a person perhaps sour in appearance, though not without reason to be firm, not without the fact that his duty was protection absolute. He was the person in the shadows and behind the walls. He was the person who was sometimes there when he was not there, perceived by students in the true form of their consciences. But he was not chiefly surreal. The deep conscience, though a comparison, really remained a different thing. Bestowed the suit of honor, he represented the tribesman chief, the knighted sir, an advertiser of the common good.

"It's true, we're sometimes slow to follow." Shoehorn explained, "I worry about being an adherent.

Look, Chief Suhr, how you're still in school."

"I know. This is my twentieth school year, but it keeps me on task. I do side with you," Shoehorn.

"I side with you too."

"Then let's both get there on time."

Once Chief Suhr headed away, Pineapple announced, "Boy, does he have our number."

"I so look forward to these powwows with Chief Suhr!"

Pineapple addressed a few more words to Shoehorn, and then he parted. Homeroom exemplified another mesmerizing movement into wishy-washy humdrum.

Pineapple emerged from homeroom with renewed commitment to hurrying. He found his girlfriend, waiting by his locker. The dress on her, a checkerboard of red and black, voluptuous like her other features of cheeks, verecund, and lips, vermeil, and youth, verdant, and veins, verditer, surfaced so his eyes might drink her like a Slurpee, so side by her side he might wag his eyes like a black-eyed puppy. She wondered why his lips were blue.

"Did some girl rub off on you?"

"Oh, no—a fist kissed my lips black and blue."

She rolled a fist and balanced it under his chin. "You eat popsicles."

"My eyes drink you, looking so beautiful in tie and dress."

"You're honest and hungry."

Pineapple stared, and Frock embarrassedly twirled.

"No," Pineapple covered for himself.

"Yes," Frock assured.

"Yes," Pineapple spoke on condition.

"Yes."

"Affirmative."

"Yea."

"Yahoo!"

"Yikes! A Yahoo isn't what you think it is. Yahoos are the bad people in *Gulliver's Travels*."

"It worked all right for an internet typhoon."

"It's true that words digress and change meaning."

"But my words for you don't digress," Pineapple promised. "Though, I'll be so embarrassed to honestly say again… how cute you look in that dress."

"Field hockey is today. We have an away game."

"Aw, naw, stay. I mean, I want to go, but I want to stay."

"Your friends will be staying, right?"

"Yes, they probably will."

She lifted his head, glided her chin over his shaven face, and with her fingers pulled a small tuft of missed chin hair. To his parted hair she flitted her hand to adjust the strands. "Pineapple."

"Frock."

"I hoped you'd call me that today." She circled her arms around his neck, leaning her head into his shoulder. "It makes me sound like one of your friends."

The tingling sensation hit Pineapple. His fingers, like beefy, bouncy, boisterous tentacles, sinking into her flesh, braced her skin. Tentacles, because he recognized only the signal from his head to grasp her and these hands that gripped her. Tentacles, as though these arms physically possessed attachment to his head, the only working parts he had while the rest of his body melted into an invertebrate mass of mushy feeling. Packaged in a large membrane, he leaned the rest of his body against hers. The differences between his flesh and her flesh he measured in the degree separations of body temperature, the sweat of her skin, and the coping of her standing strength as he submitted to her. He could not do this alone, or at least he did not appreciate his body enough.

The bell rang again. Steamy, intense, impatient—desperate, that's what the pining Pineapple was. He lifted her skirt insignificant inches and suggested, "Let's skip class."

Frock understood that parting meant starting class and too much else. She answered, "I can't do that. I have to look out for you."

"For that you're wonderful. Frock, how can you girls be so much more patient and responsible in the matters of… sex," he muttered.

"We're not, but we have to be," she answered once more.

"You girls are also more lucky to be touchy-feely. I'm going to miss you later this day when you play field hockey, and… I'm selfish."

"You think only of your actions."

Pineapple raised his eyes, gazing at last equal to her eyes, and she hugged him once more. "See, you're patient," he finished, realizing he could not keep her more.

So the gravity of school classes sucked Pineapple back into oblivion. Standing on the edge of this black hole, he endured the time that slowly packaged and processed the class subject matter away into the vault of one small part of his mind.

When his mind later resurfaced, hungry for the cafeteria lunches that beat competitors by forbidding competition, he sauntered jaggedly down the hallway, reaching the band room. Descending his arm on a mobile chair and pushing it away, he called across the empty band room, "Shoehorn, we're outta here!"

"Wait." Organizing the drum kettles, tambourine, and the like, Shoehorn sorted through all the percussion instruments.

Then, oscillating and maneuvering over the trial of a trail toward Pineapple, empty of people but littered by chairs and stands, he approximated his position and then fell. He stood up. Shoving a few more chairs aside, he met Pineapple.

"Well! Swell!" Shoehorn interjected. "You missed it. We played 'Bolero.' Quite a composition by a man named Ravel."

"You listen to classical music?"

"I play it! Anything under the sky entertains an

audience in its performance: an oboe, a viola, a guitar, a trash can, the bowels, a landing meteorite."

Scholarly Shoehorn expounded music, hopping from disco to jazz and from Chinese to Irish music and from musicians to speechless Pineapple. Disparaged, Shoehorn dropped the subject. Pineapple did not mean harm but simply subsided in the hollow of Frock's absence. With the spirited arrival of Cantaloupe later this day, new energy compelled Pineapple to entertain the subject anew in the presence of Shoehorn.

"What do you want to tell me about music?" Cantaloupe asks.

Shoehorn dropped his eyes and scraped his foot across the sidewalk. "Pineapple, it's no big deal."

"What? You were so passionate about it."

"Music rules the world! You better believe it." Shoehorn pivoted toward Pineapple. "Everything's explained."

Now Pineapple's eyes drooped as he clarified, "Dang, I didn't mean harm."

"Hey, Pineapple. Ostentatious!"

Cantaloupe looked skyward and annunciated, "Ostentatious."

"It's like therapy, ostentatious. You can't even read it! You have to say it! Ostentatious! Ostentatious! Ostentatious!"

"Ostentatious ostentation." Pineapple grinned and declared, "Ostentatious! … Ostentatious!"

"Swank."

"Swanky."

"Swagger."

"Ostentatious!"

"Well, is it a day?"

"Yeah," Pineapple observed. "We don't go to the movies often enough—do high schoolers actually do these things?"

"High school is what we make it to be, right?"

"Sure, you can sit in the corner of classrooms all day, think that and become that," Cantaloupe answered Shoehorn, "until you stand up and start wandering around. We have classrooms and rules. We have adolescence, and this sometimes leads to thinking of adulthood. The title of an independent is an option on the tax form, but depending on home's situation, dependency, it's thoroughly us."

"Minors do what they want," Pineapple invented. "That's the genius. They escape most laws and are considered ignorant in court procedures, despite the fact that they're sometimes passionate about what they're doing. That much is unfortunate, and we shun such malfeasance, though it's sometimes labeled to our broad youthful term."

"Not all high schoolers are minors. Privileges come with the turn of the sixteenth and eighteenth years. In high school I've done my work in the world to afford a silver truck. I can drive us to the theatres."

"You don't bring it to school," Shoehorn noted.

"Not while it's in the shop, but I can drive us there

this evening."

"Ostentatious!"

Plans for the evening blossomed like a flower. Then the pickup truck blew the picked flower away.

Between Cantaloupe and Pineapple, Shoehorn analyzed, "The reason for the simile is so people can compare experiences in conversation, remaining in the spirit of their comrade's experience while explaining their own. For example, if Pineapple related the horrible time he had when pimples spurted from his upper brow, Cantaloupe wouldn't have to sympathize but could explain, that's like the time when one on my neck secreted pus."

"Shoehorn, settle!" Pineapple commanded.

Slipping his hand over his bruised Cantaloupe, The Cantaloupe urged, "Leave the blotch of blood at the top of this head alone. I banged my head against the door."

War scar, Shoehorn smoldered. "I just wonder how far one can go. 'The female of the dog'—that one actually exists in the dictionary. The dictionary also cites another meaning for this word, and not slang either, identifying 'a bad or bad-tempered woman.' It suggests that these animals must exist. And Mom uses it, and Dad uses it, and the man down the street uses it too."

"This civilian has a plea," Pineapple unveiled.

"The concept exists, and so does the reality. What if I want to use the other word. You know, the other 'bad' word."

"For shame! It's just a sham," Pineapple related. "The shamed are the humbled. Shame shuns sham. The humble shun pride. Of course, the fateful honest truth—any truth, really—supercedes a curse. Bah! Let it impact not. Curses are disgruntled lies. Truth sees beyond it."

"What we attach the fowl word to and whether or not it avenges the name determines the ultimate punishment," Cantaloupe added.

"Sexual intercourse," Shoehorn declared. "It's six syllables—too many! I need one syllable or how can I be acute—severe and short, cut and clean?"

"We prefer tact," Cantaloupe pressed.

"What's this deviation from the male sex organ into fish nouns? Porgy! Ha! Poor John! Surmullet! That's not acute. It delays everybody from finding out what two people are laughing at. Just say it!"

"You're not going to," Pineapple hinted toward Shoehorn.

"You're right. I'm not going to."

"Then why do you argue? The words are obviously bad."

"These things exist! Ignorance won't solve them, won't even chase them away."

"What do you propose then?"

"I'm arguing just in case I ever need to be aware of what's on my body… and what's on girls' bodies, for that matter. If ever I need to know the truth, I'll remember this argument and rush words containing minimal syllables and base meanings through my mind."

"I get the picture."

"You mean we're going to see a picture."

"Here we are," Cantaloupe revealed.

"I knew you were going to say that," Shoehorn complained. "You said that at almost the same time and in almost the same way that I said it. Jinx! Larynx! Pharynx! Sphinx!"

"You're loaded with curses today," Pineapple spotted.

Shoehorn meditated. "Curse the picture word. We're *moving* cut and clean to the *movie*, so let's see which one, now that here we are," Shoehorn mocked.

"What a blow," Cantaloupe retaliated.

"I'm sorry, Cantaloupe. Thank you for the ride. Please trust my sincerity. I even have to add 'please' to be trustworthy after that," Shoehorn apportioned in reparations.

"You can thank me by paying your share."

Out with his wallet and out with theirs too they approached the box where they slipped the money through a small opening. Between Pineapple, Shoehorn, and Cantaloupe a standoff ensued on whether to see *Henrietta Bonbon*, *Monkeys Scratching Armpits*, or *Havoc Three*. A factor of fastest availability for the showing and who drove them here determined the choice of the third movie.

Red carpeting introduced them to fairy land. Glittery signs and gasoline-priced sweets greeted them, guided them to movie land.

Shoehorn turned back, pleading for the other movie. "Don't you have pity on your ape ancestors?"

"This way, Shoehorn," Pineapple redirected him. "A love story is tempting too. However, Cantaloupe drove us here, and he chose" *Havoc Three.*

Reluctantly, Shoehorn scuffled at Cantaloupe's heels.

Stumbling strides that they aimed down the aisle of the movie room diminished, hesitant against the dimness until they found the yellow threads of floor lights. Cantaloupe threw them toward the bright screen until incalculably they pivoted on a point along the stretch, and then he followed them, marching across the line of chairs to their seats where they plopped down.

"As we've missed a little, the good guy and the bad guy's henchmen already introduced themselves," Pineapple asserted. "We'll know the bad guy soon. Then people will die."

"Don't spoil it—I haven't seen the movie yet," Cantaloupe alerted.

"It's the formula for such a movie as this, and I'm taking a guess."

They waited for the plot to build and hatred to mount, and upon the first tragic death, the screen flashed the red of blood. The Pineapple crumpled forward as though injured.

"The acting is too good! The actor is too human!"

"Shh," Cantaloupe addressed Pineapple. "Hey.

Look there."

To where he pointed, the shadow of a head lifted at the screen, absorbing every flashing color in its proximity.

"That's Stroodle! How'd he get here?" Shoehorn posed.

Ambling along, Stroodle would intersect their lives only under these most unwarranted circumstances. Entering a shoe store one of these times ago, Cantaloupe came for boots but meanwhile encountered Stroodle, buying the same bland shoes he already wore. After a school function, Pineapple walked to the nearest store just to find Stroodle, unwinding with a cigarette on the sidewalk outside there. Shoehorn crossed one busy local street only to discover Stroodle, crossing the other way. Turning the silver quarter year, Stroodle exhumed his motion for an equal share in life if not for providence alone. He fared long, un-hippie-like hair and disagreed with associating himself to any social class. No mentioned job, except for the assurance of his industry; no stated mode of travel, except in his resourceful resilience with the public, its people, its telephones, and its privileges; and no boasted status would do. Only his visible, unchangeable appearance with the possibility to betray him presented him with slightly above average height, portraying the lankiness in his stroll.

"He's the hodge-podge of a philosopher, philanthropist, and couch potato; he's the combination of a passerby, a bystander, but a stand-out, stand fast, stand pat—an out-of-the-way fastidious pathfinder," Shoehorn theorized.

"I think one or two things contradict there," Cantaloupe established.

"It's how all these characteristics work together. He meanders steadfast and just. Despite limited human influence, he actualizes who he can attend and who he must let be."

While they talked about Stroodle, he moved away from them.

"Of course we only talk about him. While he's here, we should meet him—where'd he go?"

Out of the hazy atmosphere the red light of the exit sign sculpted Stroodle's face as there he goes.

"He's leaving! We must hurry and follow him," Pineapple directed.

"Exactly what I was explaining," Shoehorn assured.

Tossing Cantaloupe into the aisle, Pineapple disbanded his absorption into the screen and darted that way, and Cantaloupe's resentment subsided into the thrill of pursuit, so he followed while Shoehorn clumsily directed hobbling hops over the seats to faster reach them and the exit door. Emerging outside where the brick wall stood tall, they rediscovered Stroodle, who coolly leaned against the cemented bricks and tapped into a cigarette.

"Stroodle!" Shoehorn burst.

Unleashing the smoke from his mouth, Stroodle snapped, "Don't smoke. It'll kill you."

"You smoke," Cantaloupe retorted.

"It's already killing me, just like other things, killing me slowly."

"What could get you Stroodle? You're twenty-five," Pineapple pinpointed.

Stroodle laughed wryly, coughing out the smoke. "I should've guessed. You want to know. Ah-em! Third time to this movie, and I still can't get beyond the first death scene."

"It's just a movie, and we can gladly be removed from it. It's not real," Cantaloupe defended.

"Of course it's real. It's symbolically real. Someone really intended it. Some audience needs it. Because the director created awareness of suffering, now I have to save the world." Stroodle bit into the cigarette. The tip glowed, and he blew the smoke away. "What's putting you down, Pineapple, Shoehorn, Cantaloupe? What are you trying to earn into? A lover?"

"School fears blame and thus blames us, and they're right because they're law," Pineapple cited.

"That is a scared lover."

"They protect us, we understand, but they don't always sympathize with tardiness or revelry. Restrictions they place on unruly students they also place on us. We suffer them, but to little avail." Pineapple vented with a final puff, "Your life is so different."

"How do you propose my life has changed so much from yours? Presently, neither one of us are in school. You're affected by the economy as much as I am right now."

"Stroodle, what's the meaning of life?" Shoehorn surged.

"Here. Now," Stroodle shortly responded, limply dangling the cigarette. "Get a job. Get a life."

"There has to be more."

"You have too much respect. That's why you're still searching for life's meaning. You have to earn into it." Stroodle tapped the cigarette, and pieces of the burnt end flurried. "It makes sense. You can't win over a million men, and there are billions to put you down. You can't simply flaunt your humanity, so patiently, respectfully you apply yourself for such an ability, even sacrificing bits of yourself along the way. So the wind sculpts you. So water wears you down. So the sands of time grind you." Stroodle lifted the cigarette but halted his shaking hand. "Of course, then you come back and think it's something about feeling. Well, it is your feeling and nobody else's. Otherwise, you won't change those who don't want to be changed, kings or criminals. You had to apply yourself. Application. Respect."

"Your dictionary never dies. That's what I think," Shoehorn suggested.

"Sure. Concepts like Rome exist. They never die."

"Concepts like evil exist."

"So does good. In addition, your dictionary suggests word function, such as verb and noun agreement, but doesn't mandate a formula for every sentence. I would meander to elaborate on the attachment of words to sentences to the tenses to life—life goes right back to the beginning of words. While I deviate, you're correct, Shoehorn, and should remain firm." Stroodle gave up on the cigarette, dropping it, and stamped it into the blacktop. "Did you friends ask for a conversation?"

"He asked for life's meaning," Cantaloupe aided his memory.

"Oh. I still can't get that damn movie's death scene out of my head. No substitutions, fellas," Stroodle wished them, jaunting along the long brick wall.

"Goodbye!"

Stroodle waved every goodbye with his hand past the backside of his head of long hair.

"With Stroodle gone, how should we get back in?" Pineapple vacillated, "Should we sneak back in?"

"Wrong kind of thinking," Cantaloupe determined. "We have our proofs of purchase. We'll show them our tickets and reenter up front."

As he with them watched further death scenes, Shoehorn regressed to the primary scene of death that Stroodle could not fathom. The irritation enlarged like a bump on his head so that when he slammed against the bed, nightmares could ensue from the terror. Movies Shoehorn remembered like *Robo Cop* and even the acclaimed *Apocalypse Now* flaunted death, staging people falling out of windows and rolling their decapitated heads, scenes providing little justice for the overkill that glorified special effects. In waking he shivered, despite the warmth of the covers, regardless of his cozy clothing as he ushered to the bus in early morning cold. From bus to school Pineapple would invigorate Shoehorn with demands subjugating the day and praying on the position that crazy was an opinion. Cantaloupe joined the pressure on Shoehorn, but preoccupation with death bred defeat in his mind. Then he got that blow to his shoulder and swirled around, face-to-face with Big Teeth.

His henchmen assailed Cantaloupe and Pineapple by throwing them against the wall. Cantaloupe jeered, and his opponent wobbled backward. Pineapple stylishly danced his palms around his adversary, dizzying him. Shoehorn did nothing, and Big Teeth jarred Shoehorn into the wall.

"You parade down these hallways like an animal circus," Big Teeth walloped in laughter. "Watch the horse whinny! Watch the chimpanzee scratch! See what there isn't to see—wimps! Apparently you are the weakest of all," he singled out Shoehorn, shoving his shoulder.

"Fight back," Pineapple advised.

Shoehorn separated from the wall, disinclined to make revenge a compensation for brash injustice. "Big Teeth!" Shoehorn abruptly interjected, lashing his teeth. "You menace! There are rules you bend. Here's one you break with voice cracking, lips flapping, and teeth splitting your gums!"

"Air-sucking weasel!" Big Teeth sputtered. "You spineless walking lump of jelly!" Big Teeth wound up, but Shoehorn avoided the fist that cracked against the wall. "Aaaaah!"

"What's going on here?"

"Big Suhr!" Pineapple gasped.

"Did you hear what he called you?"

"Enough," Big Suhr instructed Big Teeth. "I saw what you and your friends did. You're in big trouble."

"But you didn't hear the name they called me!"

Big Teeth, "these are good kids. If they address you with a name, it probably fits. Now put a cap on it! You are all coming to my office."

Stifling any snickers, they watched Big Suhr lead Big Teeth and his accomplices away.

"Big Suhr is on our side," Pineapple beamed. "Big Teeth got what he deserved!"

"Big Teeth isn't the worst of it."

"Of course Big Teeth is bad. Shoehorn! Not only does he represent corrupt humanity, he *deliberately* practices ill acts."

"That much is unfortunate and ill-received by us," Cantaloupe elucidated.

Shoehorn sulked and swung his foot aside from them. "Nevermind."

Shifting concerns to his friend's disconcerted face, Pineapple implored, "What is it, Shoehorn? I'm done for now."

"You can tell us," Cantaloupe assured.

Reading them with his eyes, Shoehorn informed, "This really will be the end of it."

Pineapple gestured for him to proceed. Cantaloupe twitched his shoulders, hinged his elbows, and nurtured his knuckles in anticipation of something drastic.

Shoehorn drew them aside and dropped his backpack off back. Unzipping it on the floor and reaching in, he ripped out a history textbook and flashed it in the air. Ink etchings, crafted on the textbook cover, promoted hidden meaning. These were words, indicating more depth than mere broad black slashes and wide ovals turning sharp corners. Adorned with autographs, phone numbers, people's wills, this book cover was a souvenir that the owner must save if he valued what this year's high school life was worth.

Sweeping his hand beneath the cover, Shoehorn threw the book wide open. Locating the specific picture, Shoehorn flaunted the page, displaying it for all to see, angling it to neighboring bodies, cracking the binding to further expose the image. The casualty of war without gun or armor lamented every inkling of his pain. Shoehorn covered the victim's eyes, and now the only cry for help emerged from his mouth. Uncovering the eyes, Shoehorn concealed the mouth and body beneath. Now he gazed at you, but you did not know why. Exposing the man's body while pressing his thumb over the man's head, the result in Pineapple and Cantaloupe was bafflement, for the form was so utterly inhuman without the hollows of eyes and mouth, making the body a lump of excess, bloody flesh.

Furiously flipping through the pages, Shoehorn now revealed that soldiers grappled on the lines of battle. The dirt smothered their blood and tears. Pineapple staggered, suddenly suspicious of the surrounding school's stagnant atmosphere.

More pages blew aside. Shoehorn tossed them, and he presented another page with presidents, prime ministers, demigods, visionaries. Peaceably they negotiated the means to eliminate atrocity. Cantaloupe stepped forward to make one point. This specific frame hosted the Big Four at WWI's end, victors who could not devise a treaty over their enemies to prevent a second world war. Shoehorn would skip through the pages to the victors' compromise at WWII's end or Nixon's peaceful negotiations in the Cold War with Zhou Enlai; the pages would fly, unveiling German soldiers, French soldiers, American soldiers, Korean soldiers, Vietnamese soldiers; a bloodied baby wailed over the bombed Shanghai train station or the Holocaust or the documented napalm and human flesh in the Vietnam War.

A dramatic thwap ensued. The textbook graffiti covered up the inhumanity. Shoehorn returned his book to his backpack, zipped it, and hoisted it upon his back. Pineapple scoured the hallway for the impression this spectacle must have caused, but students and adults passed nonchalantly by, either unfamiliar or unresolved in this display. Cantaloupe persisted in the notion of atrocities while continuing the motion of perpetual forward ambulation, detached from the fixed position in which a still picture often captivated its viewer. Pineapple, Shoehorn, and Cantaloupe distinguished the part of inhumanity in humanity. What mattered were the viewpoints they took on these things of life.

Pineapple nodded. Shoehorn devolved. Cantaloupe decanted. This inaction. They took that picture. To death, to pictures, they offered their celebrations of life, for more than this offering supplicated that an unabated amount of tears must water the earth, so more than this they absorbed it, not offering a final opinion but stirring in the thought breeding thoughts as life intended. Animation surreal. Pineapple, Shoehorn, and Cantaloupe looked into each other's eyes. They checked each other's mouths and bodies. They were the living. They will not create their own casualty. They will not make casualties. They will respect life.

The Cantaloupe

It's all the same, spinning round, all over now, such that has been. I stayed the course of a day, hit a rut, fell into a trench ten miles long, never knowing where it began and I ended. I've been a man to myself but not among others, bobbing my head in and out of gunfire. The general should have scalped me before sending me to their war. Peeping carcasses of beer cans, discarded pillows, unwrapped Tostitoes, barely a place to rest my head, these inventions of peacetime wartime have me stuck in the barracks of Suburbia. Heavy artillery, Grade A shooting. I never had so much fun in the third grade. If they sent me to their war, their foreign exchange student with guns ablazing, they'd blow apart all emotion until I was a man, destroying me before the enemy blew me away. I'm tripping over magazines of pictures, white uniform condiments, an unemptied trash

*can of another war-torn vacation. Daily
I greet civilians who are barely teenagers
anymore, though I remember that time
most true. The teenagers I see are
eighteen and nineteen-year-old adults I
mistake for kids. Eighteen, nineteen,
legally adult; teenager, adult, anomaly.
When did they cross that line to call it
sudden maturity? Bow before Colonel
Cantaloupe, whose established habit puts
a kinker in the energy drinker. You've
never seen a melon filled with more rum.*

An angular yellow ray departing from the shutters glared menacingly on Cantaloupe's head. His drooling eye procured the sunlight, but his brusque breath reintroduced the morning, raising the tail-end effects of last night's consumption into his face like a bristly skunk. Bred with yeasty alcohol, that breath could kill, but Listerine would kill first, dousing it in more alcohol.

Cantaloupe levied one arm down to get up and tripped over beer cans to move. He counted their graveyard corpses: junked, lopsided, crushed by mischance, tipped over, run over, picked apart, complete in a progression that accounted for his present headache. He was not calling it a hangover, but it was a migraine.

Walled in by the bathroom mirror, squaring his attention on his cactus-like head, Cantaloupe grimaced, swashed the Listerine and spit it out, and checked his irises before setting his eyes down upon the gray fuzz. He stuck an electric razor to it, cutting pathways to expose new skin. With shaving cream he whipped the top of his head like a cherry. With eyes rounded to detect every splinter of his movement, he plucked the hair stubs from his scalp using a different razor, rinsed, and finished his image off with a tipsy smile.

Wiping his head with his hand and detecting an unbloodied but reduced surface, his numb hand had him fooled, for the rough stubble would regrow in short time, reverting back his gray Cantaloupe. The ensuing shaving experiment on his chin and cheeks, though more attentive as he desired a kiss from a lady today, failed as well, but he smacked his rubbery face so his cheeks lifted an irreversible grin.

Cantaloupe stumbled out of the bathroom with princely pride, kicking the metal skeletons from their graveyard. He returned the glow outside with a glow his own, pausing and glowering back again. The anti-septic lining of his pickled stomach disagreed with this reinsertion into the optimist's day. Cantaloupe ditched his stupor and grew curious about the jarring door soon ajar beside the living room.

Castigating looks from furry eyebrows and this comment, "Do you think this is your living room?" jounced Cantaloupe into mistaking him for the general, but then he realized who had cowed him, the Crouton, a white cracker at best.

Cantaloupe convened, "It's my weekend lease.

My friend released me from wandering the plain. I thought this was Suburbia, where a man could trash his home as he pleased."

"You don't please me. And it's my home. We're in College Town, and it's a dry campus."

"Which means nothing when it rains."

"You trash yourself and have the audacity to trash my home!"

The beer cans glinting like a defeated army at dawn lodged indiscriminantly between corners, cushions, carpeting. Overlooking all but the leaking corpses as true casualties from last night's binge, Cantaloupe returned dismissive eyes to a stern face with its blond head of hair squared off, flaunting a flat top. Cantaloupe would compromise this difficulty with his friend, using THE name, "Crouton—"

"Clean it up, Cantaloupe. Think I approve because every underage person does it?"

"You can beer or not beer—"

"Not here, you can't!"

"—but get lucky in College Town."

The door opened wider for a black man who emerged, greeting The Crouton, "Good morning, racist!" Scaling his brown arm up the door frame, he tapped its surface and repeated, "Good morning—racist!"

Observing his manner, accompanied by fixating but vacant eyes, Crouton descried, "Don't tell me you were drinking too."

"Nah, I won't, racist."

"I don't discriminate by race but by age, and you're underage."

"Well then… what say you, age-ist?"

"Don't try," Cantaloupe intervened. "Why, Afro Biscuits could walk a straight line a mile long."

Turning eyes on Cantaloupe, the name man said, "Hey, leave 'Afro' out of it. And you know what I said about stealing our other word."

Cantaloupe gesticulated at his head. "I have a fro."

"But you don't have that word. That's our word."

"'Our?'"

"Well then, both you clean up this mess," Crouton concluded, his face souring like a pinkening mold that highlighted the whiskers on his face. Noting that the spotty chin gave his friend's stale face extra garlicy texture, Cantaloupe buried a snicker. It wasn't right, Cantaloupe deemed, that THE name described the entire shape of the head, not the haircut alone (and a square chin?), allowing for the attraction around the faculties of reason and emotion.

Braiding his palm-leaf hair back into their braids, Biscuits's eyes absconded from Crouton with a plummeting gaze. Crouton nearly marched past him but cast off, "And I am not a racist!"

Biscuits observed, "That doesn't influence my view or my word for you." Discerning that Crouton looked ready to eject something awful, he amended, "But hey, I call all my white friends that."

"Then who's really racist?"

Biscuits shook the defilement off with his beady, bouncy hair. "Aw. You need a hug."

"I'll take that nap. I didn't wake up right," Crouton admitted toward Cantaloupe, "but you two better clean that up before I return," Crouton deferred in final abdication.

With sharp-edged shoulders, arms, and a slouching stomach, Cantaloupe saluted Crouton before the door closed. Cantaloupe dwindled his arm back by his side, and Biscuits released a smile. "Is he serious?"

Cantaloupe responded, "Well, he crashed our party."

"We finished it last night, but it barely began. I can't believe you can't get your other friend in on this, or how about The Shoehorn? I'm really surprised he doesn't turn out to drink."

"He doesn't drink."

Biscuits chastised this admission, folding up his large arms and countering, "He's doing something, wouldn't you say? Otherwise, he'll try something."

"I don't know what you mean."

"Ask him sometime. Everyone does something. Even your friend Pineapple smokes. Where do you think he is now but on break? At least that's not so uncommon."

"He's trying to give that up."

"Once again, not so uncommon."

"But Shoehorn is clean."

"Clean when he takes a shower in the morning. Do you think anyone retains their innocence? My parents saved up mine with their discipline. That's how I'm here in college."

"And innocence doesn't amount to anything anymore when life is a party. Cash in," Cantaloupe instructed, lifting a cylindrical beer can and crushing it. Hurling the can, he watched it bank off the trash can rim and cycle a few centimeters across the floor.

"You can't blame me for making fun of you white types when your actions imply your shortcomings," Biscuits suggested regarding that lonely can on the floor.

Cantaloupe surveyed his friend. "Are you part of the college experience I haven't paid for, purporting the word 'Afro' to me when all my culture wills me to name hairstyles 'fros' and then stealing both words back from me?"

"Diversity isn't just in color," Biscuits professed. "Understand the hairstyle. Besides that, we're too similar."

"I could've said the same thing, but coming from you, it's different."

Biscuits looked offended, huddled up in his brown body.

"Don't get me wrong. I just don't think it's such a big deal."

"And that's our problem, that we don't make it our concern."

Cantaloupe let out a grunt. "Problems. Don't talk

to me about problems. There are problems with every beer can on the floor that's not enough. You and I must drink plenty beer to provide enough scrap metal to power a hundred electric shavers."

"You can't make me believe you've tried powering an electric shaver that way."

"Don't they teach you anything here in college? Stop quibbling the same words with me and let me show you how metal can fit between the batteries."

"Metal can fit, like battering steel drums, is more how I imagine things," inserted Shoehorn, straggling out of his room.

"Go back to your graveyard of sleep," Cantaloupe bestowed.

"This is the graveyard of commotion that kept me awake. At least your drinking put you under eventually."

"Don't remind me. Rapture punishes, leaving me low."

"How much do you plan on partying tonight? We have to drive out of here tomorrow."

"We can always call in sick Monday."

"Not much has changed since high school, has it?"

"Yet it has. When was there ever this much freedom and nothing to do with it? Everyone drifted apart since high school. Freedom leads its disillusionment."

"Maybe half of them remain here at college," Biscuits suggested.

"There's more economy to be made without

them."

"Working for others."

"We should be starting over with family, but many aren't that quick. Most of us wait to exchange true freedom. Age will rebuke our hesitancy."

"It's not like we weren't learning to drive on our own back in high school," Shoehorn amended.

"What are a few rights versus the full?" Cantaloupe retorted.

"Nobody is completely free. That's society."

"I want to find a place that cannot be touched by society or its wars, susceptible entirely to nature."

"We have come far from that beginning."

"Yet we remain in this nondescript vapid landscape where people lie in wait among the bushes."

"What about their liberation that is natural, such as by their promiscuity?"

"By that, there is no end to whom we ignore like boys running over flowers in a neighbor's yard." Cantaloupe raised his arm and swung it forward like he was throwing a football. "What are we doing but proving ourselves when instead there should be nothing we have to prove? Man is a shout into the void."

"It issues from a source. It may not echo back its reason like it does when we rap at the walls of local authority, but there is man capable of counting the hairs he has yet to shave. Man is at the center for his universe."

"That is known. Then what is fancy versus

frolicking?"

"The same."

"We have not dispersed far from the tree that dropped us in our predisposition. Each self hoards his hill of beans now for the winter of our lives. Should we ever see a spring again, or are we more focused on making children than children we have been?"

"That is the cycle. Only Pineapple has deferred the real world for the welfare of education."

"What welfare is there besides learning of the world one withholds himself from experiencing? Where is that schooling boy anyway?"

"He must have gone outside for his equivalent of a coffee break."

"Then let's a round make around where he went to ascertain his hiatus."

Cantaloupe and Shoehorn bounded for the long stemming balcony from the doorway, and Biscuits chided, "Doesn't somebody need to clean up all these beer cans?"

"The enlistment of help is necessary," Cantaloupe responded on his way.

Smokes of a pathfinding habit stream over the banister and up into the unimpeded atmosphere to mix with vacuous negations of dispersing air particles before making the clouds. Pineapple holds his breath before each puff as to stomach the smoky form he later molds into humans absconding late in this life, prior to the child he imagines to birth as from within.

"That must be the longest cigarette to outlast the confusion of this morning," Cantaloupe relayed.

Pineapple exhaled visible breath and spouted, "It should have lasted longer if there had been someone to whom I could talk."

"Don't let it kill you."

Pineapple pointed, "How is that different from life, slowly killing me?"

"Smoking kills faster."

"That's debatable. Smoking forces me to slow down, but I see your point. I am trying to quit."

"Why is it that a smoker seeks fresh air in order to fill his lungs with garbage?"

"He wouldn't, but others keep him out of doors. Smokers do need their communal space set apart, though."

"We come to visit THE friend in College Town, and he has already ducked out on us," Shoehorn belabored the point.

"I hoped Frock would make it here soon. She's a regular here on Saturdays. Either that, or I visit her at her College Town."

"Apart, yet never closer together," Cantaloupe surmised.

"That's the years, where we grow together." Pineapple drew a long smoke. "There's nothing to do in this College Town."

"We could chance getting past security at a bar."

"That's overrated. So are frat parties. Who really

wants to dance all night?"

Shoehorn put out one forearm and then the other, chanting, "Dance to the—music!"

"There's College Town, and there's Town," Pineapple explained. "College Town might be responsible for half the locals during the school year, yet Town has the bowling alley."

"That's up our alley, alley-oop!" Shoehorn mocked with the dual motion of lifting and throwing a bowling ball.

"How did we manage to stay together while our worlds separated around ourselves?"

"There was no one any more interesting than us in College Town."

"No one shares our roots."

"No one remembers our struggles," Cantaloupe commissioned.

"No one fosters the need for savoring our condition. Students write their own schedules, buy their own books, and are not us two," Shoehorn demonstrated of Cantaloupe and himself. "With more freedom, there is less capability for rebellion. Where is reaction to simple day?"

"People rally for some serious causes on campus, whether it's the protests or protest papers."

"It's not the same as when it's all in the same spirit, one as in teenage rebellion. Even the Goths some day nod to the punks. Adults are nonconforming and off each other's base."

"We'll be stuck in the barracks all day unless we go into town," Cantaloupe reasoned.

"Easy for you to say," Pineapple described, flicking and stamping his cigarette. "You've hardly given me a break by coming here. I should get out of town, much less College Town, to some other town where they for sure don't know me, particularly by their roster. To know me is to test me."

"I'm sure your girlfriend will do that. Here she comes!" Cantaloupe foretold.

Radiating like an actor, Frock appeared from stage left to tackle Pineapple into a hug in her ambition. Frock leaned into Pineapple for a kiss. "How is my butter cakes, my honey muffins?" Pineapple implored.

"You know I'm your one and only Frock," she chimed.

Pineapple nodded away from her. "How foolish of me. It is I who am your suckling bottom-feeding lovey dovey."

"I will have none of that. We meet. We kiss." Frock kissed him again and then tilted her head at a side. "Smoking?"

"I was. You know I'm trying to quit." Frock smothered him this time with a hug. "Why couldn't we meet at your campus?"

Frock beamed, "You know these are your friends, who wanted you here. Besides, I get another chance to meet your roomies."

"We were in the heat of reconnaissance. I was

under active duty to recruit for clearing a mine field," Cantaloupe remembered. "It seems I got a bit off track."

"What is he talking about?" Frock inquired to Pineapple.

Cantaloupe paced where they followed, and he swung the door open to a clean room. Baffled though Cantaloupe was, Biscuits explained, "Someone had to do it. It looks like that someone was going to have to be me."

"I see. Then why don't you awaken the private with your report? Besides, I think we were all about to go someplace."

"Wherever there is to go," Shoehorn condescended.

"Why don't we eat out?" Frock proposed.

"There is no eating out in this town without eating in," Pineapple realized.

"All the same, I think we could stand to get some brain food. Get your friend—"

"Crouton."

"That's the one. We'll add him to our soup." In Frock's car and Cantaloupe's truck, the three plus Frock with Biscuits and Crouton cruised to the nearest diner to make a bill. Nobody was modest among the equal-sized entrees to order. Frock rallied, "I had a little difficulty getting over here because I ran out of some of my makeup this morning. I had to make a pass at the store."

"You would have not chuckled the least to see what almost held us up this morning, although neither did

I get that nap," Crouton grumbled.

"Make a day full from early rising," Shoehorn figured.

"It was Biscuits who cleaned up the trashy floor," Cantaloupe weighed in.

"Really?" Crouton returned.

"I couldn't make even my first rim shot. Leave it up to him to call out all the shots."

"What did I say about being racist?" Biscuits mentioned.

"I paid you a compliment."

"It was in kind, but it's less of a commendation than you think it is. I picked up the cans, placing them one at a time in the trash receptacle like any white cracker once discarded them in the first place."

"Whatever keeps us out of trouble."

Pineapple pawed a biscuit and descried, "Now, I think you've all met my Frock."

"We have," Biscuits agreed.

"She's a bit teased today to be more than a Frock, though really, she is more than what she seems," Pineapple inspired her, "even when she's all that she seems that's just—amazing."

"I can't believe I got talked into getting stuffed into this joint. We should be solicitors outside," Cantaloupe determined.

"I don't think they want any here."

"This is the proper way to do business," Frock ventured.

"Yes, but now we must compete for a window seat to know the open world, unlike if we were parking lot dummies," Shoehorn spotted.

"There are enough of us to be seated and intimate."

"As long as I do not have to become inmate for a day."

"Have a seat, my man," Biscuits offered. "I was getting tired of looking at all those crackers in the parking lot anyway." Biscuits got up.

As Shoehorn switched with him, Shoehorn prescribed, "Who's the racist?"

"I am afraid sometimes I have been taught what I am taught." Biscuits sat back down.

Shoehorn plummeted down and spouted, "I suppose we are to blame much as your leaders forfeited your forefathers a continent away."

"No, I could not blame you. Only so many of you are Saltine. There is no need today to say anything about it, though we do it out of habit or memory."

"I hardly recognize you apart from the bunch."

"You take me to be a banana-swinging ape?"

Shoehorn shook his head. "You would abscond from me for being so base and derogatory."

Pineapple tapped a finger, adding a duo to the table and then a chorus of all his strumming fingers. The food arrived, plates surrounding the largest table of the mid-shift meal of the day. They were capable of ignoring their differences in dietary choices as they carried on.

"My insurance rate on the truck is coming down," Cantaloupe imparted.

"Imagine," Pineapple investigated, "if we remained in high school, we would have no need to pursue insurance rates on vehicles, much less search for our middle meal of the day as it is. Government like the education it puts forward affords us protection."

"Are you saying our hides are exposed?"

"As to the public, it is true. No longer are we surrounded by the many same ones as ourselves. At least it is not a choice made for us, though I do spend my time mainly accompanied by peers on weekdays as almost a coincidence."

"It seems part of the system preserves itself if so much remains the same."

"It's inertia, spinning in space, but it can't last much longer. Either I grow old here or get out into the real world eventually. Besides, we must pass through town to College Town on vehicles our own."

"That is a difference."

"There is a lot more to worry about," Shoehorn assimilated. "Have you ever thought about wanting release?"

"Abandon we may experience by a sugar high, but what would you suggest, a runner's high where we tear up the miles by our own persistence?"

"Those remain controlling factors. I mean release from control, abandonment of security, even."

"No, I don't know that I've thought about it. I

keep on as I am. What brings it up for you?"

"I want something to take the edge off of worrying, release from the pain, release from the care."

"Perhaps what you need is a good tea," Frock suggested.

"At least it's not smoking or drinking. It's not like I long to light up or drown my cares. I don't want to feel exposed or depressed with whatever I do. I want to feel happy like euphoria. It doesn't get any easier, being adult. There's hardly a way out anymore."

"We are no longer under the care of our parents or principals," Crouton understood. "One shackle at a time, society unbinds us. For some of us there remains provided us a walking stick to carry because still there is education before all that must go straight but high."

"I can't stomach it myself. What's to take the edge off of reality?"

"You want a lollipop?" Biscuits offered.

"I've had enough not to care for one anymore."

"That's how it goes with a lot of things, except love," Frock inspected, toying with the curls on Pineapple's hair.

"You get accustomed to something, then outgrow it," Cantaloupe considered.

"That's life for me now," Shoehorn confirmed.

"Such a terrible thing to say," Frock exasperated. "You can't mean it."

"After life's small triumphs, there remain the impurities of melancholy. I wonder how to sort them out in the bottom of my cup."

"You would not know who you are anymore if you drank enough," Cantaloupe convened.

"That's the idea, but I don't drink."

"What got us on this somber topic anyway?" Pineapple apportioned into the scenario. "Of course we all bleed until we stop it up, but the human form exists in perfection when without any of that strain, I believe. It's more how to sort through the nit-picky things society has against us with ideas to taunt us toward freedom that baits us on to where we must insist the emperor has no clothes or the cheese smells alone."

"It's like how we must pledge allegiance to the flag," Cantaloupe elaborated, "with our hands over our hearts like we were only Napoleons with our overcoats."

"Or like random cartwheels that upset the walking and talking," Shoehorn fomented.

"He has it! Life is all normal until we rationalize our stake in dyslexic ventures. Raise your right hand but only to pat your comrade on the back in commiseration that anything had to be done."

The waiter raised his hand to refill glasses, including Pineapple's own, and Pineapple relayed, "All this talk did have me thirsty."

"Are you enjoying your meals?" the waiter asked.

"Splendid! Terrific," Pineapple answered for several. In renewed absence of the waiter, Pineapple purported, "These workers remind us of where we are headed."

"Much less where some of us already are," Cantaloupe reminded him.

"There remain those with their seniority in years. We are fledglings, but closer to the real world than we've ever been before with little turning back. These live people sport real jobs, this sum being employed for everybody, unlike the old lunch ladies, whom we never could become."

"It was our place to become janitors."

"Not if I can help it while these others appear upon us from every direction."

"It's like if College Town didn't work out, there's still the Town," Biscuits spotted.

"I hope not. I'm like a tiddlywink about to be snapped to any distant square for my vast learning. All sorts of employers will need me."

"For that most basic of readily available education," Crouton cited.

"It is I who will have earned it, which is not so much a concern as that I do go. What then? Someday, most pressing will be the prospects. How will I fill in the empty space of losing teachers and peers to bosses and associates? By the end of my life, there will be the extra rests at the end of a song. That's retirement from a job sluggish to get there, forgetting the showoffy overture. The necessary rests have me just as much out of breath. The vigor of our days eventually shed years without interest, so left behind. I cannot fathom it, how I climb a ladder to no mountaintop. I rise up, yet the only way forward seems to return back down, but that is no option upon a continuum as life. I must learn to fly."

"We spend much of our time guided by parents as well, but that does not mean we all will soon be without them. They expect the third generation."

"They hound to enact for us what they only could enact once for themselves. It is us who began to walk. It's like a complicated chain in billiards where I hope not to strike and sink last the black ball."

"What do you have against blackness?" Biscuits interceded.

"I was thinking about a black death. Things end there—but things need not end here between us if you remain hot on some issue."

"You are all ghosts to normalcy."

"I cue it at the moment, but it is important that the game sports a black ball."

"Sure."

"Will time leave us behind to die as it must be in this game, or will substance yet remain like the game ever is played again."

"You know where the black ball goes, direct in the center for the rack."

"Where will we be but standing on the green when the golf ball goes sailing into the clouds?" Crouton figured.

"I don't know about you," Biscuits resorted back upon the issue, "but I yet prefer a traditional end with the black ball."

"Where will we be someday, Frock?" Pineapple enticed.

"We'll have a home of our own," Frock depicted, "with kids dancing around a quiet garden. That garden will be for me mainly but also for the children to learn steady, sturdy hands. It will be our getaway from society at large in Suburbia."

"Sounds like a plan, our haven in heaven, the two of us plus a family. Sure you'll come to visit," Pineapple beamed out.

"How could we possibly circumvent the chase? We'll be pounding on your door to get in!" Cantaloupe pictured.

"That is if you don't have quiet homes for yourselves by that time." Pineapple believed he might have started a family with Frock by now, but promises to their parents to complete college delayed that, not that he expected he could sweeten this deal any further.

"One can always hope." Everyone prepared for their reabsorption into College Town as though few had shifted from the amniotic sac of education. Pineapple patted his pant pockets. "It seems I'm out of cigarettes."

"What ever will you do?"

"I'd hate to recollect everyone over to the gas station when we were already on our way. People will tend to get strung out if I unleash ourselves there."

"I'll go," Cantaloupe offered. "To the corner market down the road. You've got the greater carrying capacity in Frock's car. Matter of fact, you can take everyone else. I'll go it alone."

Pineapple bestowed a hand to his friend's shoulder. "Cantaloupe."

"The. No, don't worry about it. I know where you live. I'm sure you'll be there." Cantaloupe waved, and then light as a bird, he flew down the street to the only gas station in town. He piled out of his truck and sauntered inside direct to the cash register where an array of cigarette packs broadcast at him. "Excuse me, do you have something royal-sounding in cigarettes to encourage my friend to quit, like he'd finally realize what a sourpuss he is? Naw," Cantaloupe naysayed, batting the air, "That would just be a bonus effect, a byproduct of elevating him to where he must look down upon himself all silly."

"Why don't you use your own eyes to look?" the cashier with his back turned spouted.

Cantaloupe grimaced but explained, "I only ask because you work here."

"Yeah? What of it?" The cashier turned, and Cantaloupe found himself face to face with an old nemesis.

"Big Teeth? What are you doing in Pineapple's College Town?"

"Didn't he tell you?" Big Teeth shifted out his bottom row of teeth, nearly as big as the top. "That doesn't surprise me, but I'm outside his jurisdiction where he is student."

"I just thought that—"

"I'm surprised you thought."

It was like consorting with an enemy who in the least was adversary, who concentrated most on his own next move, which Cantaloupe was not about to provide for him. "I suppose it doesn't matter which cigarettes I buy for Pineapple."

"That's more like it. They're all the same."

The door burst open with a gunman. "Hands up! This is a robbery! You too, cheeky boy. I want to see those hands!" the robber declared. Cantaloupe and Big Teeth obliged. Big Teeth's legs shook. "You, put money in the bag."

"What bag?" Big Teeth inquired.

"Any bag! Get me a bag, and put the money in it."

Big teeth scrambled to obey. Once he filled a plastic bag full of cash, the robber fled, and Big Teeth crouched in a corner with his butt flagging. "He wasted no time," admitted Cantaloupe, who heard an automobile squeal away. It was the grudge and grunge of people taking advantage of others from out of the shadows, which constituted the precipice before which he dangled, where society's draining residue was to evil and spite. He was about to slide down into this upheaval until the robber grew indifferent to them, though it was not before making the situation dangerous to all for his smalltime gain. School zones differed. Students were protected from all but themselves. Now Cantaloupe realized he had filtered from there into the general community that could threaten the life out of him for a daily business. The chance had always been there. Cantaloupe made the emergency call and then told Big Teeth, "I'm going to wait in my truck for the police to arrive. I don't think you have anyone else—certainly not him—to fear."

Big Teeth, looking behind himself, recollected himself at the cash register and exacted, "Of course."

"Just ring up these cigarettes first." Big Teeth performed his duty, and after he rung it up, Cantaloupe provided, "Keep the change."

Cantaloupe maneuvered about his truck less emphatically than he imagined the criminal had abandoned for his vehicle, and he threaded a forefinger under his nose. He had been useless, utterly useless. If the outskirts of Suburbia was his war zone, he was no more than a woman or child in it, though he might have justified his self-defense to act. Instead, he escaped for near certainty with his life, not the target of this game, a spectator to a crime that would not either cost the cashier his job. Yet it unsettled him, the threats on their lives, in what could have been a complacent town.

When the police officer arrived, Cantaloupe out of his truck explained everything he could. "He wore a black ski mask, was taller than me…" The cop was not last to arrive.

"Cantaloupe," Pineapple applied himself, "where have you been?"

"What's this about a Cantaloupe?" the officer implicated.

"He is THE Cantaloupe—a nickname provided

him."

The officer nodded and stated, "You're lucky to get away. Thank goodness you managed to stay calm in there."

"What is he talking about?"

"There was a robbery," Cantaloupe cut in for the cop. A baby in a nearby car wailed. "Big Teeth was the victim."

"Did you owe him slack?"

"Unpleasant though he may have been when I walked in, he was the one wronged."

Pineapple nodded as Frock repaired to his side. The baby wailed again. "Oh, look at the cute baby," Frock said to the lady holding her child in her car. "He's not quite a Cantaloupe."

"Nope," Pineapple vented. "He's Peach Fuzz."

"Do you think it's safe to go in?" the mother asked.

"I was just reporting," Cantaloupe conveyed, "for a crime that's past. It's perfectly safe with an officer here."

"I wouldn't, but we're in dire need of supplies," the mother determined, heading in with her child.

"We were worried about you," Frock explained.

"It was a holdup," Cantaloupe ordained. "Society is not without its pitfalls. I always thought it would happen while I was at work."

"Such a shame people have to steal and endanger lives in the process."

"They're effective that way, not that this is truly effective for society or the betterment of mankind," Cantaloupe decided, getting into his truck, which Pineapple patted before going for Frock's vehicle.

It took Cantaloupe a while, unable to reassess his situation at the gas station, before he realized Pineapple and Frock traveled without Shoehorn, but he figured it had been in their hurry. That was until they too seemed surprised about Shoehorn's utter disappearance back at the place. "Have you seen Shoehorn?" Pineapple interrogated Biscuits.

"Should I have?" Biscuits cited. "Shoehorn is getting to be a bit of a big boy to be telling all the time where he goes."

"He usually would tell us if he went somewhere."

"You hardly said a word before you left."

"I figured you might have guessed I went to check up on Cantaloupe by this time, who had a run-in with a robber."

"Ouch. Did he turn out all right?"

"He and the cashier made it out unharmed—but where is Shoehorn?"

"I saw Shoehorn stumble off for the room at the end of the hallway," Crouton added into the conversation.

"What hallway?" Cantaloupe intervened.

"This hallway, here."

"It's more of a walkway, wouldn't you say?"

"Either way, that's where he went."

"You didn't stop him?" Pineapple's voice rose to

a scolding tone. "Those people are getting into trouble a lot."

"I suppose I didn't. Shoehorn must've figured he wanted to be with a more rowdy bunch tonight."

Pineapple chased after Shoehorn with deliberate steps while Cantaloupe and Frock pursued. Pineapple pushed the door to the party straight open. Because of the loud rap music and people necking, no one seemed to notice the newcomers. Bumbling over and around people, Pineapple eventually spotted Shoehorn in the corner with his head limp. "Shoehorn, are you all right?" Pineapple inquired. Lifeless Shoehorn demonstrated splayed legs and a ghostly outlook. Pineapple smacked him on his cheek. "Come to!" Shoehorn let out a groan. "He's still conscious," Pineapple reported. "Did you take drugs?"

"Oh," Shoehorn moaned, "don't tell, anyone…"

"We've got to get you out of here. Lend me a hand," Pineapple importuned to Cantaloupe. "Upsy-gosey!" They carried Shoehorn out with one arm slung over each of his friend's shoulders. By the time they reached back to Crouton and Biscuits, Pineapple seemed ashamed yet boiling. "They let you do this to yourself. We would never let you do such a thing. Was it too much for you? Were we too much for you today? Answer me, Shoehorn! You couldn't have liked those people very much, particularly with their music. Too strangling." Hunkered against the wall, Shoehorn snoozed audibly.

"Is he going to make it?" Cantaloupe asked.

"I think so. He's tired is all, but I'll keep watch over him all the same." Pineapple vaguely remembered the earlier conversation Shoehorn entertained today. He could not imagine this as the abandon Shoehorn desired, capitulating into an eventual uneven sleep. Much as Cantaloupe worked himself out of danger, Shoehorn applied himself for it. What they were coming to was a precipice of adult abandonment of responsibility or feasibility no less. Temptation made no exemption of victims to those surrounding the principle example in straying.

Frock

The woman of today is business and add-ons like cell phones and appliances. She is seven different layers of mascara and fine clothing. Decipher her mood by her gait. If she walks with one foot in front of the other, swinging her legs out the side as to catch her balance, follow along the rope walk with her. If she trips, that means she was looking, an embarrassment to women trying to prevent notice with side-long glances. When it seems like she's going somewhere in a hurry, she probably is. Women budget side dishes and accounts better than men. It is why women carry so much from the folding mirror to the hair pin. A women feels her shoulders upon which others stand by her flowing hair. If you could see her neck, it would be like looking up her ankles without the blemish of effort or a stain of sunlight. Her demeanor is reserved and unrefined like queens never abdicated their thrones. Her talk is the talk of the town, and her purse is her secret, a well of industry and modernity. She hops in and out of traffic while evading alleys, alley cat though she is without a man around whom to curl her arms. She will outdistance even him if she has more than a hundred dollars in her checkbook and a free day, not that it is likely in her enterprising realm until the after hours of the workweek.

Frock suspended in her chair with a dome dryer overhead. She read the latest trendy magazine, imagining herself where she was not, on a boat or balcony. Fashion was the accoutrement of tomorrow, and one was never wearing it if not accompanied by a red carpet. A woman shopped for tomorrow, and when she walked from the mall, it was like a car leaving the lot. The clothing she secured depreciated heavily upon leaving, weighing her arm down where it had lifted to a mannequin. Frock turned a page of her magazine, uncrossed and crossed her legs the other way. She looked from left to right, top to bottom. What she needed was a pedicure to complement the sponginess her hair was to attain. That, and another several grand for holiday. She had been to Venice and Paris, but what Moscow women wore these days she pondered to set a trend for an early winter.

On either side of Frock sat Lasagna and Celery, who went by Sanya and Ree, though their designations best defined them, Lasagna with red wavy curls and Celery with perfect long blond hair. Of course Shoehorn and Cantaloupe provided them with their appellatives, which they claimed so long as they took a knee to using nicknames instead of supplying their full-blown sugar-coated appetites to whet their lips. Sanya flipped through her magazine like she was sensitive to the arts, for not all nerds were uninsightful, relying upon what academics already knew. They could suggest plaid shirts or khakis any day. She wore auburn plaid over her chest like she left the checkers tournament for the resort Jacuzzi. It was this artificial paradise of tanning salons and hotels she appraised. All she required was a plane to live between locales like an apostrophe between key letters, which she outgrew like a butterfly that darts left and right while moving forward.

As for Ree, she steadied on the photo of a Miami woman in bikini. The legs and arms were pure two by fours, but the chest and hips screamed for caresses like from a hawking beach guard. A bowl nestled its fruit. The eyes hid by shades like she otherwise would turn her observer to stone with a look, for she was a gem to earth like lightning   to sky. Ree had hair like any model woman, so Ree did not feel outmatched, though she could go for a patch of sand on the shore.

The women were on break from college, grooming themselves for festivities to come. Sanya tried not to bat an eye, for she would have to dab it with her finger. Ree poised like she were carried on the shoulders of men. Frock blinked at the safe face to society, a slathering of colors and a template of frozen identity. Everybody in the magazine was white as her, fraught with cares for minute corners of the human body to clothe, expose, or ornament. It was a world beguiling the outshining sun by a smartly placed hat or an umbrella or an awning. Frock ruminated over whether it was natural or someone must try to be really white, privileged by genes to secure face beyond what cosmetics could do. She would rather be like a peach anyway, succulent from the touch of her blushing skin. With her girlfriends, she did not try for anything, but then there was her Pineapple.

Frock tried shades beyond the rainbow, but never had she settled upon black. She would not appear gothic, which she must to wear black explicitly. She could not identify its culture of loathing to herself. If she was anything black, she was bold, not beholden to her shadow. Neither could she be white and black, the gangster colors of the nun. There was everything in-between, yellow like a canary and pink like a succulent flower. She attempted sky blue and emerald. There was anything but to stay one shade, half shirt and half skirt or pants. Even shirts had become baggy as of late, but she preferred to reveal her contours like a book cover, tight to edge. Her clothing should be sharp as her smile, but there must remain room to breathe, for it got hot to trot on high heels.

Women lived to be told what to do when it was how to appear or act. They must seem ladylike and don crushing smiles under similar clothing. Frock liked being a woman, which she deemed one must only after putting up with all the applications of eye shadow, lipstick, and earrings. She did not feel like she was put up to being a Christmas tree, more like the queen. Every woman received certain hair and body differences from the others, and she must work it. It did not matter if clothing sizes numbered out to a hundred. A woman must make it fit. Then she could run or have the waves splash against her like any free man.

Glancing beside her, Frock entertained a funny thought, that they were to have their brains interchanged via the dome dryers. It was common for women to live vicariously the others' lives through conversations and hugs. What was surprisingly uncommon was to possess another woman's body. A woman must dress different to be the show of the day. What fit one woman did not fit another, but they were equal in empathy. Frock wagered if she were Sanya, she would dance with her curls. If she were Ree, she would drape her long hair over banisters so men knew immediately they were on the lookout for a sharp blond. Then she could read their magazines since she had extinguished the highlights of hers. She could go for an angle on a man smiling like a wolf or a woman looking up to her plane away. Beside these peculiarities, Frock could not be anyone else, for she doubted she could convince her empire to follow her without her wardrobe.

Ree looked to her hair stylist. Ree had asked her to cut her hair the least of the women. She fidgeted to be consoled as a child neglected of the attention that should be so common. The hair stylist smiled on her in passing like everything would be all right, but Ree felt like a project under the dome, about to become the Frankenstein of bad hair days.

Sanya forgot about the dome dryer entirely, wrapped around an existence of stale smiles posed to photographers whose eyes focused down to earth to reveal a human, not some wig thrown over a faceless plastic head. Uncertain how they lived so close to these otherworlds, sitting or running in them, Sanya bobbed her head all the same like she required sleep. What these women served to parchment Sanya broadcast down the street, a woman to be sucked up from the roots of society where she was in action, not changing her clothes throughout the day for the montage of her catalogue. Sanya would be bigger than the sign for the local coffee shop once she clopped her high heels and swung her plastered face against the clouds like she walked off the pedestal in a clothing store, about to turn heads requiring a sign for wholeness like a shell sticking partially out of the sand.

Frock looked up to where the buzz issued from the dome dryer like she was to be abducted by a UFO. It was enough to live by others' suggestions for more or less makeup, but not being able to see the machine above her head set her on edge. She imagined they were to be throwbacks to another era before it was all over.

Ree closed her magazine like she used part of a napkin. "How am I supposed to see these articles and advertisements about what men are to buy me? I don't know what age one should be to own a Cadillac," Ree mused.

"It's not outside my budget," Frock doted, thumbing to another page.

"Unless Pineapple buys you a necklace, how can you expect to pick one out for yourself? He'll think you have admirers."

"How about a bracelet instead?" Sanya suggested.

"That's a sure-fire way of indicating to everyone that you're someone else's baby."

"So what if I am?" Frock laughed it off. "We can't expect not to indulge ourselves every once in a while, but a ring not granted is most confusing to men."

"Why does society dictate what to wear? I can't try on sandals before it's spring or a sweater before it's winter."

"That's the weather," Sanya indicated.

"You know what I mean."

"There's nothing but to try," Frock speculated. "Why not be daring so one may set the trend? You can be an omen of spring or a portent of winter."

"I like to wear sweaters when it rains."

"There will only be people telling you not to wear them."

"I'm okay with that."

The stylist hatched them from their shells. Their hair held in place, spongy when they turned for the door. They waited outside for their intersection with the men. Frock had as much of an idea as the rest of them to where they spun if not to meet the gals directly. Each of the women toted a purse to match her personality. Ree's purse was a little black bag, indicating she had no idea of what to choose for herself since it did not match her denim jacket. Sanya's purse was the opposite, an off-white that hid in walls when she left it to idle. Frock chose her purse to be a blistering red, woman that she was. The women looked well-defended as the rays warmed their ankles.

Ree spat, "Why do we have to wait around for the men?"

"It's their choice of concert," Frock realized. "Shoehorn wanted us to go."

"So men are choosing for us." Ree dwindled, "Imagine if a man didn't know what to pick out for his woman? I would hate that. The difference between pink and white and black and tan is a delicate issue."

"You can always coax him to shop around with you."

"Besides," Sanya intervened, "when do you see black or tan?"

"When he wears it," Ree bestowed. "It's in the pants."

"So you are choosing for your man?"

"I should if we are to match. Imagine if he

walked into a restaurant with burgundy and me, a canary yellow. It would clash worse than dirt on sand!"

"I don't know that's so uncommon."

"It's like banana and kiwi in the same fruit bowl. Are they even from the same climate?"

"I believe that they are."

"Probably not the same island."

Frock distinguished Cantaloupe's truck rising above the other vehicles. She waved, and Sanya chided, "His truck is white. Is that okay with you?"

"It is," Ree assured. "Can't go much more neutral than white."

Pineapple glimpsed out the passenger window with a smile while Cantaloupe pulled up to stop. "Ladies," Pineapple greeted, "I see you're fit with your new trims."

"I feel much lighter," Frock chirped, not knowing what to say.

Sanya awkwardly put in, "You can't cut out these curls."

"They look so twirlable," Shoehorn cast past Pineapple with a glance around. Sanya twirled her flashy red curls to show it was true.

"Did Ree survive?" Cantaloupe inquired. "She's not a powderpuff?"

"What's that supposed to mean?" Ree triggered.

"I wasn't sure if it was going to be a perm."

"It dries like all other hair."

"The concert is an hour away," Shoehorn

remarked, throwing up his hands. "We have to get there."

"All you men concern yourselves about is going."

Shoehorn snapped back into his seat. "What's that supposed to mean?"

"We've been having a bit of a conversation before you showed up to entertain ourselves," Frock put Shoehorn in the know.

"Lady stuff," Pineapple imparted beside him, "which appears mainly to be about men."

Frock danced her bangs in place. "How can we resist your self-centered worlds?"

"If only we had a thing to do before converging with you, my sweet." Frock poked her head over the sidewalk, and Pineapple and Frock nuzzled noses. Pineapple looked down his nose, able to see her feet from the vehicle while Sanya and Ree glanced away as though distracted. Sanya continued to twirl her hair. Pineapple unwound, "You look pretty."

"Oh, stop," Ree inserted for Frock.

"They barely began," Sanya amended.

"Don't encourage them. I've seen Pineapple and Frock forget they had anybody there like the world existed for them."

"It's young love."

"I feel that way about my drums," Shoehorn impacted. "I start drumming, and it's like nobody's there, though the music's happening."

"It could happen in the desert," Cantaloupe surmised. "The heat gets to you, and you start seeing things."

"It's opposite for them," Shoehorn envisioned. "They're not seeing things."

"You'd feel different if you were hung dry, like after seeing an oasis, you'd forget yourself, tearing off your shirt and running without shoes."

"Maybe this summer," Pineapple determined. "I can take you guys anywhere, but we're lucky to have this troupe off their hiatus."

"It's not like we didn't have anything better to do," Ree supplied.

"I don't know what six makes but the whole pack," Sanya allotted.

"A shame we couldn't jam you in here with us," Shoehorn mused.

"My hair gets curly enough when I sleep on it."

"Yeah, I'm with Frock," Ree courted her. The women giggled as though Ree had named it. They skirted to Frock's car, and only Frock waved behind her.

"Age doesn't change women a bit," Shoehorn supported.

"Does it change any of us?" Cantaloupe defended.

"I thought we had not escaped the benevolence of our youth," Pineapple chastised themselves.

"We wear the laurels around our heads like wreaths around our necks," Shoehorn cornered. "It's difficult to know when the ground elevates us."

"But a green collar is all the rage," Cantaloupe attested. "No sense in staying green behind the ears."

"That's what you people say," Pineapple allotted. "I'm going to live forever."

"That's a long time to stay old."

"You'll be young until you have someone to call you old."

"We'll work something out."

Entertainment goers dotted the landscape at intervals like these were stragglers before forming the line and eventually the patches of watchers before the stage, the mecca of rock 'n' roll. When everyone reconvened, Ree asked, "Are they going to sing all about love?"

"What rock group, being young, does not take it up sometime?" Cantaloupe addressed.

"A movie date makes sense to remind us of love, but I wonder how angry these young people are."

"The Pretenders are sensitive to all," Shoehorn named his band. "They might sing about love, but they have a theme."

"That's what love is, pretending," Ree commissioned.

"It takes belief to be captured," Sanya idealized.

"I doubt it since they are Pretenders. Lovers are sincere," Pineapple begged.

"It takes an imagination to keep the romance going," Frock purported.

"No less when a person must imagine one is more."

"But you are," Frock bestowed.

"How can these two do anything without each

other?" Ree protested. "At least to us, going to a rock concert could be normal."

Pineapple and Frock chuckled like children. They were no less together in line, and Cantaloupe and Shoehorn stood behind Ree and Sanya. Cantaloupe ordained, "It was your idea."

"We'll make the most of it, but the Pretenders are like any other band," Shoehorn imparted.

"Not extraordinary?"

"You can say that is an art not to try to be, typical as life, so you feel them in your bones. I can't guarantee there won't be a love song."

"Who could expect otherwise?"

"If they were more of a punk band, though they might fawn all the more, there could be more rebellion than conformity of love."

"I don't know if they'll fit our standard. Ours is a cause in which we believe without hegemony. It is unnecessary to stand in our way when we mean not to put others out of their way."

"But we ask that they open their eyes," Shoehorn encited. "A fledgling with an open heart is nothing to be taken for granted."

"Nor is a young man racing a pony down the street with a bouquet in hand."

"The way of all things may be toward love."

"Not if he was thrown them for winning the local marathon."

Ree excited to Sanya, "It must be more of a guy

thing to go to a rock concert."

"Not really," Sanya returned, "though these are men performing."

"Men have all the doing, but ask one what he thinks and it's like putting him on the spot."

"I can think of stores that would not exist without us."

"As though things were only to exist for us," Ree huffed. "We exist for sandals and short skirts and necklaces."

"There is nothing wrong with that. It is only ordinary."

"Pineapple and his friends are all about the extraordinary, ostentation and the outlandish, but I think I'd scream before seeing them dance through a muddy puddle."

"They would do it to feel alive."

"I'm as much alive when I see in the mirror at home what others saw during the day."

"They are scared much would change."

"I can live without knowing what others think. Who knows? They may have their hearts invested in the authority that supercedes them."

Funneling through the gate and pushing through the crowd, they encroached toward the stage. Everybody faced forward like they were in a theater, though they were outside. When a guitar wailed, the audience knew it was underway. A voice above the air carried to their ears:

Fool me, mock me,
Play with my little heart.
Say it wasn't the last
While you flew.
Play with my beating heart.

The bass drum thudded to provide a heartbeat, pulsing through the viewers and into their chests. Pineapple and his crew were to sport little to say that could be heard, though they peered into each other's faces. Particularly Shoehorn snared them to make sure they were catching the groove.

What did you say
    In the first place?
But what did you mean
    In the first case?
What do you say,
    To forget?
What would it mean
    To forgive?
Move over
    If you care,
Or take my place
    If you dare.

Ree nodded her head forward, but not to the tempo. She knew it would be a love song. If only she could hear her breathing, she might pump it into Shoehorn's face, but he cared the least of them, totally into it, shaking his head and wrestling his arms while bowing toward the ground. Even when it was not hard rock, it was rock to Shoehorn. He was sure the drummer disciplined the singer to keep it poetic, no more than eight beats permissible in a measure, usually no more than four.

Cantaloupe broadcast the melon of his head at the stage, precluding what it meant to forget or forgive when facts were hard existence. Transgressions were not easily forgotten, and one must forgo his impulses toward being wronged once to forgive. Living vicariously asked for much when one could not be sure who oneself was in the mirror. Cantaloupe weighed that Pineapple and Frock must have made concessions to stay who they are. Cantaloupe only feared what it meant to be understood while it was difficult to be heard in the first place.

You know,
You're not so special.

The Pretenders went crazy, flaring their instruments and thrusting their hair over their faces. Shoehorn outdid them, pushing into the crowd so he was forward and back, propelling off a back and then a chest, sidestepping into Cantaloupe and Ree. Cantaloupe caught the drift and started pushing too, cautious about the women. Once the crowd separated from Shoehorn and

Cantaloupe where a step was no progress toward anyone, they broke into a jig, kicking their feet at each other and thrusting their arms before spinning round and around.

And you know,
You're not something special after all.

The guitar chord banged, and Shoehorn collapsed with a leg in the air. As though reaching for a hand, Cantaloupe pulled the leg so Shoehorn uprighted himself upon it. Ree looked affronted toward Shoehorn until she saw his Mohawk dabbling over his forehead. She stifled a giggle, and Shoehorn smushed it back into place. Sanya observed the climate change in Ree, but Sanya put it upon Cantaloupe that everything was back in control. They would not have to carry the boys out after all.

The crowd resumed its incoherence if it noticed Shoehorn and Cantaloupe at all, but a stoner prodded his reefer hand toward Shoehorn. "Dude, you should try this. It will really rip you up."

Self-aware, Shoehorn diverted a gaze toward Pineapple and Cantaloupe. Shoehorn released back at the stoner, "That's not for me."

Shrugging, the smoker relinquished, "Whatever, man," before congealing back into the gathering.

Cantaloupe socked Shoehorn in the shoulder. "I know who I'm with," Shoehorn reflected, thrusting his head thoughtfully at Cantaloupe, "and I mean what I say."

"We know you do," Cantaloupe assured.

For the remainder of the performance, the Pretenders paraded on stage more than even Shoehorn or Cantaloupe swayed in the aggregate. When the rock band concluded, people did not leave like they expected an encore, but they received only the drummer back on stage, who thunked his drums but waved a peace sign before walking back off the side. The women perched beside the men like birds, unsure of what to do. Pineapple stole his arm around Frock and preached, "Let's get out of here."

Draining through the gates with others, Pineapple and his band evacuated the premesis. "They're heartbroken with a touch of punk," Ree explained.

"It is inescapable to consider love," Cantaloupe ordained with a hand stroking above his head like he had any hair. "The Pretenders see love for what it is, a charade, much like them, invented purely in the mind."

"That's not what real love is, but I'm not going to say it's always about the romance."

"When there is no one left to love," Shoehorn intervened, "the Pretenders cannot leave themselves to love, for they see their smallness."

"They're like any other band," Sanya decided.

"Give them the glory of a few lines to outweigh them all," Pineapple considered.

"It's like Zen," Frock input, "short and sweet, but you must laugh through their struggle, how they must care about anything."

They arrived in the parking lot. Like a concert of cars, vehicles surrounded on all sides like gumballs in a gumball machine, but Cantaloupe and Frock had their picks. Without paying another dime, they rolled from the collection with Cantaloupe leading. Cantaloupe settled his arm where the window lifted with his hand pinching the roof. Pineapple as the support between them raised, "It's one of the many diversions we face, that rock concert."

"It's not every day a person gets his music live," Shoehorn declared.

"You make it sound like strangling a turkey," Cantaloupe purported.

"It has every chance to remain alive in our memory," Pineapple supplemented.

"The purchases don't stop, either," Shoehorn rectified. "I'll have to buy their album."

"You cannot buy the day," Cantaloupe seasoned.

"There is many a moment to collect."

"It's amazing our homes remain enough to house all our memories through life."

"That's after we throw much of the junk away."

"What if it is not all that way? There's plenty I save."

"You may have lost things without knowing."

"It's not even that. You couldn't live in all the garbage you're putting out, so it is too much."

"What if our thinking is simply too small?"

"Here's the 'What if' man."

"All I have to say is, so?"

"I'm saying we cannot know how upright we might walk if our homes were large enough to suit the bodies of adult men."

"It has come to this."

"We are adult."

"But young until we feel different."

"There are too many to look down their noses at us."

"It is not without our grins that they look down their noses to find the nuisance of our tandem bicycle tricky wheels in their driveway."

Shoehorn watched the parking lot and the stage go out of sight. He noted they took a different route, probably to avoid traffic. The truck and car veered in half circles up an incline until they ushered on top. The view of the concert was once again complete but on high and from a distance. Shoehorn waved and commanded, "Stop here."

Cantaloupe thought it was nothing more than a child's gesticulation, but Cantaloupe saw the berm large enough for two cars to park. Frock crept up behind them as they pulled to the side, and they all got out.

People like ants before a stage like an anthill centralized in the expanse. Shoehorn observed the cars crawling single file out of the parking lot. They left in time to be early. Cantaloupe perceived how much land remained to be converted to settle the population, and that land that was cultivated provided a patchwork. Frock and her girlfriends joined shortly behind the men, who stood over the barrier beside the road like it was the edge of a balcony.

"Say goodbye one last time," Ree enjoined.

"Pretenders, how much we knew your hard rock 'n' roll," Shoehorn patronized.

"The stage will remain here for forever that we know to host them once more."

"Rock music is a young person's game. We can only pray that they stay together."

Ree swiveled to Shoehorn, glancing straight-edged. "What does the future hold for us? Frock and Pineapple have invested their future."

"We stitch into the present," Pineapple remarked, interlocking the fingers of one hand with the hand of Frock.

"What if we don't have a future before a child, whose future is forever upon our minds?"

"You will be that much more in the present awareness of your offspring's company," Cantaloupe reasoned.

"The prospect of a child's safety forces it," Sanya compounded.

"I can't imagine a future beyond where I'm going," Ree speculated, "but that's what it is, a series of adversities we have yet to take on, some that don't seem rational at the moment, like retiring."

"That's a far bet," Cantaloupe gasped.

"I barely know what I'm doing a lot of the time,"

Sanya supplied.

"The future doesn't have to make sense now," Pineapple invoked. "Imagine us trying to make sense of the past, but it's impossible not to think of what could be better. It is a natural progression like we could only grow up. That is direction, reaching without grasping like a mime or a salesman, who works for his day, yet it is to accommodate others. This symbiosis is the same for us, born of a society of apish ancestors, yet look at our improvements, which are suggestions beyond the wheel: the recliner, potato gun, and stretchy spandex."

"It's difficult not to think of myself buried by my future," Ree explained with a hand to her eye.

Cantaloupe steadied upon Ree, "It's like putting on slacks, but take it one day at a time."

"What if I wear a skirt?"

"Then you have only today," Shoehorn envisioned.

"That's not so bad," Sanya consoled Ree, brushing a hand up and down Ree's shoulder.

Ree stared at the stage that appeared overbearing, despite its distance, swallowing her like a cave. She advanced, "Memories indicate the future more than anything we know. We stockpile this investment, believing we will look back one day, knowing where we've been, finally somebody." Ree sheltered her mouth with her fingers. No more speculation, she watched the stagnant atmosphere for a sign, any change to split the firmament, but there were only the unhinged pivots of her friends to esteem without gaining upon her. In existence affirming memories, she entrusted there was more than a past that had never been or a present without lending moments unto others. Without a shell to shed or any gift of accoutrement into which she must grow, she had arrived without feeling older.

Stroodle

A day arose like any other. Cars whistled down sidewinding streets. City dwellers navigated the grid, angling along corners like they were auxiliary to entire buildings. The city rise blocked the sun rising until it glanced in sideways, a real Peeping Tom. Children ran down streets. Couples marched together. There could have been anything that was not, but no carnival through here went unprepared. No futuristic car tantalized like its sheen. War was a foreigner, despite their lives of quiet suffering. When it was sunny, it overshadowed them, though the light abided unchanging into afternoon.

Stroodle awoke with a hunch, pushing against the mattress. Light flooded his body, though it was as the moon. Stroodle had his hair entangled, though it strained straight and long. Self-straightening, it never required more than to sunder from pillow, the mold of his dreaming.

His feet touched the floor, and he looked out sliding glass doors to the city. He felt naked as day. He did not ask to be called Stroodle, but it had been happening for so long, he never protested, nor did he call anyone less than their deserved names. Children were fighting over a ball in a neighboring yard. Stroodle flinched at the sun ascending. Day was ahead of him. It should renew the search for a woman, upward mobility in a career, or a croissant. Stroodle relented on what the day provided him, first a hot bath. There must not be much to figure, or man would not have survived by pastry alone.

To the transparency, Stroodle strode after kicking into his slippers. He unclasped the door to his elevated porch, and the sun burned his shoulder. He tried to make out the violence, the owner of the ball and who demanded it, but they were sticks short one handle. Only a need for the ball justified claim, as did their sport. Trucks whizzed by, everyone with somewhere to go. Only birds rested on a wire, enamored of it all. The broken phrases of their song were crippled by a vexing breeze.

Stroodle lit a cigarette, cupping his palm with intent. Smoking made the victim precarious until the nicotine swelled in the lungs. Shirtless, Stroodle received the inner warmth. He was a smokestack among shanties, nowhere near uptown or the outskirts. Stroodle liked to think people who rented here lived between their futures and upbringings. It was a step into the city for everyone with gusto to walk there.

Buildings rose like a mecca. The symbol being phallus, earth did not deny. Then nature forgave shortcomings, all except this cool blue sky. It had been singed.

Stroodle clasped the cigarette near his chin. A day was upon him where it would not be enough. His aspirations were not what they should be, being simple and solitary. Provided he spent that silver quarter year, people expected him to be something different.

To the counter, Stroodle sprung and floated his cigarette upon an ash tray. The walls stared back at him. Empty whites dangled him in open windows. No portrait compromised their gloss. Stroodle cracked a hard-boiled egg where he did it secretively and snuck a glance out of doors. Bookshelf and desk floated a room away, but he kept it real. Flowers were for women, and guys had dolls for women. He watched whole days flee him as this egg without a care. He was at peace for a man with everything to gain, not to count out additional cutlery and cooking pots. The walls turned inside-out wherever Stroodle saw himself a short distance from escape.

Pacing each hour with every cup of coffee firing his blood, as it was, Stroodle drowned the urgency for another cigarette. The walls were scleras where Stroodle aimed his look like in a museum.

A school system once served him. Now society expected his work to afford his tab, however he found it, which was wherever he could land a cigarette stub in tight corners. The earth was borne steadily beneath him, but somehow, it did not matter. Born with inalienable rights of the living, Stroodle respired where he could. He might live for others, but debt was unnatural. His own foiled spectacle was in waking without care. Daylight resisted urgency. Night was under duress, but he could pop his shoulders from the stress, a string bean loose to let innerness reign.

His mother had seen good in him. His father had been hard, the backbone the family expected. Anything else was imaginary. Stroodle felt animalistic urges where it was necessary. He did not feel plastic, nor trammeled. What he felt was hampered among his peers. They were chicken ivy. Every day should be so individual as itself.

Children retraced indoors as the day wore itself. They suffered the strain. A ball remained in the yard with a lost cat. Stroodle slipped doorside and lit another cigarette. A cop siren wailed in a city transfiguring. Stroodle followed it indeterminately. A siren seldom reached its destination, just its turn. Then the stretcher pulled. Stroodle could hear that one go.

A chill air glanced inside through the door crack. Stroodle felt disgusted at it not being reason enough to pull on a shirt. He was in sweatpants besides. It was nothing self-conscious as stubbing his cigarette into his thumb. He robed and jacketed himself, a changed man, though pantsed to shorts. He did not necessarily agree with the weather. He could trot before the storm, should one rise. From his den, he scooted into the city.

Cars persisted in their bustle. Buildings lit up from the inside as though previously invisible. Everyone had somewhere to go.

Stroodle docked cornerside where the crosswalk sign bade him onward. Revelers here were spectacle to a city of changeless infrastructure. Tables outside made it beautiful, whereas inside, customers could choose to be cramped. The city towered, for it repelled nature as smoke. A pocket of grass near a car lot was like despair. The city blotted out the sun with awnings, which stood ready for rain. Particolored lights were almost neon. Christmas would be early again if it did not feel late.

If the elements meant to outlast Stroodle, yet was he durable in a cold shower or fog. A restaurant nearby outlasted its owner on a perpetual corner, but Stroodle awaited a gull to crap on the sidewalk like a message from above. Cigarette stubs and burger wrappers were plentiful but suitable in this fair city. Everything had an eventuality about it. Whoever had been cleaning up here needed it be the city that shone, whether or not anyone cared.

Patrons ushered outside as they had cajoled in. Stroodle allowed the bustle to drain past him as sweets on a pudding bubbling. Here was the city, he faced it at himself, with nowhere to chase this heedless chatter. Humanity at its best was boring. Everyone dressed like egg salad. Sidewalks jutted for Stroodle to observe. Traffic was the bare constant, like a toothpick. It was not that the city met Stroodle here. He endeavored where it seemed implacable, as that a Danish meet its end. A corner restaurant might someday outlast him, though the city never escape him. It alone prevailed.

The lights caught Stroodle off balance. Their swishing put the entire city in limbo.

Up from a recent intimate duo, three young men had joined. In crossing the walk that was their life, they hopped to the beat of a blinker, skipping perfunctorily by them until it happened. Three young men, forlorn and striding, swiveled glances from the middle out. Stroodle peered back from an unshakable stance.

"What, it's Stroodle," Shoehorn commissioned.

"That it is," Pineapple seconded.

"Gentlemen," Stroodle addressed them as they were. Each could be blubbering or awestruck instead of how Stroodle chose to view them. It was the hairline difference between a Shoehorn like a mohawk and parted hair for a Pineapple. Otherwise, it was how they chose to call themselves, young but inopportune, attaining age without reason.

"What brings you out this evening?" Cantaloupe asked his compatriot Stroodle, affecting a gaze at his clean shave like a cantaloupe.

"What doesn't bring me. What could I expect for yourselves?"

"We haven't any purpose but to travel," Shoehorn evaluated.

"Here in the city long enough, you figure there is a place to go."

"We're making it," Pineapple realized.

"It's not intuition that guides you. Cities are a mold," Stroodle raised.

"It's home," Cantaloupe discerned, "or home away from home."

"You're getting by like a fiasco. City was built for man."

"Nothing like a river."

Stroodle unloaded, "It's near one."

"Where should we go?" Shoehorn ventured.

"Where do you go? Are you not here?" Stroodle summoned them.

"What is to expect above expectation?" Pineapple puffed. "We're never reluctant this far in."

"Imagine staying where the adventure is over."

"Where is it by your age?"

Stroodle realized, "With young dreamers or the defeated."

"We never could wait." A Mazda squeaked up the street. It let out a whine as Pineapple let on, "What about that one? Is he young without a sense of authority to guide him?"

"Look, what countenance you bring, gray and drab. Authority is everywhere."

"Trouble is wherever it finds you," Cantaloupe stated conversely.

"Others do not differ so much from us if they wear a Pineapple, Shoehorn, or Cantaloupe," Shoehorn defended themselves.

"The hairstyles are hip that are new," Stroodle enlivened, "so you will be just a coat on a rack."

"What about your style?" Pineapple invaded. "That will never fade."

"I never knew who I was, man more than anything."

"If only we were not constantly at war with

ourselves," Cantaloupe idealized, "others might no longer seem a threat. Language and law are bridges, yet barriers. Our will to obey is not Commandment. Men have come before me to make a living past. There is no investment in the day."

"Can we put a face to feeling, or is it reason is set and unerring?" Pineapple seasoned. "How can we live with others without ourselves, for which the search continues?"

"It's like asking if waves are near or far," Shoehorn added to their conundrum. "We know how far we've come, but it is no distance to return. I cannot shake my roots, like this hair."

"Dare you beat Rapunzel," Stroodle chided.

"You win for our Rapunzel, for your hair down in this castle respite."

"It's more city than your school."

"It has not ended us," Pineapple pledged.

"It will. It must, but the question is, where will you?"

"We attempted escape," Cantaloupe reasoned. "The world awaits."

"Will you make your masquerade?" Stroodle raised to their prate that was never-ending. "Nature returns you to the earth like your skin."

"We sometime must return to earth or wherever on it. We go reluctantly, kicking our feet and swinging our arms, knowing ourselves more alive than heat."

Pineapple, Shoehorn, and Cantaloupe faced

Stroodle all this while as a tribe detecting vantage. Then they turned as though in someone's way. To see with Stroodle eyes the city bustling in declining day, they must make these streets. Free of more than the confines of a classroom, unlimited possibilities seemed to lend themselves nowhere. Business was at its center, yet it was outskirts to somewhere. How much farther to tread into the pith of human affairs they did not really know. Their searching was testament to itself, one being made with the future. Inescapable as the morrow, nothing was so settled. On an ordinary day, they expected a pale breeze to find them. Their dive into splendor remained buoyant on waves like tomorrow. Expectation was noncommittal where it was possible. A kick kept them off balance. It challenged their potential. As seeds borne in a wind, cycling the likes of they did not know where, they should fall not all at once. A hole in the ground seemed an excuse for falling. They were stand-ups for hire on a spiral toward arrangement, light-headed and swimming in a sea of class and kin. Never so aflame did a moment appear than in preparing for another.

Printed in the USA
CPSIA information can be obtained
at www.ICGtesting.com
CBHW071032121024
15668CB00066B/683

9 798330 424825